H A S E N

HASEN

A NOVEL BY

Reuben Bercovitch

NONPAREIL BOOKS

David R. Godine · Publisher

Boston

This is a Nonpareil Book first published in 1986 by
David R. Godine, Publisher, Inc.
Horticultural Hall
300 Massachusetts Avenue
Boston, Massachusetts 02115

Originally published by Alfred A. Knopf, Inc., in 1978
Copyright © 1978 by Reuben Bercovitch

Library of Congress Cataloging-in-Publication Data
Bercovitch, Reuben.
Hasen.
(Nonpareil books ; #44)
Reprint. Originally published: New York: Knopf, 1978.
I. Title. II. Series: Nonpareil book ; #44.
[PS3552.E69H37 1986]   813'.54   86-4689
ISBN 0-87923-577-2

First printing
Printed in the United States of America

For Stephen, Fred, Saul, and Marc—
these, too, were your brothers.

Notre justification, s'il en est une, est de parler pour tous ceux qui ne peuvent le faire.

—Albert Camus

H A S E N

1 Hase, 1 Tasse Hasenblut, 100 g. geräucherten Speck,
1 Zwiebel, 1 Bund Suppengrün, einige Wacholder-
beeren, Thymian, 1 Lorbeerblatt, 2 Esslöffel gehackte
Petersilie, 2 Esslöffel Butter, 1 Esslöffel Mehl, 1 Tasse
Rotwein, 1 Tasse Würfelbrühe, Salz, Pfeffer.

Man bereitet Marinade folgendermassen vor: siedendes,
mildes Essigwasser, gehacktes Suppengrün, Wacholder-
beeren, Thymian, zerdrücktes Lorbeerblatt, Petersilie, und
Zwiebelwürfel. Der gehackte Hase muss darin übernacht
marinieren.

Vor dem Zubereiten der Mahlzeit, den Hasen gut ab-
trocknen, salzen, pfeffern, und mit Speckstreifen spicken.
Dann giesst man die Marinade durch ein Sieb. Man hält
die Gewürze und Zwiebelwürfel zurück. Man fügt Mehl
dazu und lässt es dann mit Würfelbrühe bräunen. Dann
lässt man es abkühlen. Man nimmt das Fleisch und die
Sauce heraus und legt es in einen gewässerten Römertopf.
Dann giesst man Rotwein darüber. Man deckt den Topf
zu und lässt den Hasen ca. 180 Minuten bei 200° kochen.

Man nimmt den Deckel runter, giesst das Blut herein,
und lässt es dann noch 10 Minuten kochen . . .

H A R E

1 hare, 1 cup hare's blood, 100 g. smoked bacon, 1 onion,
1 bunch soup greens, some juniper berries, thyme, 1 bay
leaf, 2 tbs. chopped parsley, 2 tbs. butter, 1 tbs. flour, 1 cup
red wine, 1 cup beef broth, salt, pepper.

Prepare marinade by simmering mild vinegar, chopped
soup greens, juniper berries, thyme, crushed bay leaf,
parsley, and diced onion. Divide hare into serving pieces
and marinate overnight.

Remove meat, dry, season with salt and pepper, and
garnish with bacon strips. Separate the marinade with a
sieve. Remove spices and diced onion. Add flour, brown,
and slowly stir in the beef broth. Allow to cool. Remove
meat and sauce to presoaked earthenware pot. Pour red
wine over all. Cover and cook in 200° C oven for approxi-
mately three hours.

Remove the cover and cook for another ten minutes,
after stirring in the blood . . .

—Traditional recipe

HASEN

I

THE HARE woke at the sudden burst of the night-jar.

She quivered once, then stiffened. Again the night-jar trolled; a soft churr, not a cue of alarm.

Eased, the doe licked her forepaws and scrubbed her face. She plucked mats of fur from her belly, widening the uncovered area around her teats, and piled the tufts beside the truss of fresh grass. Then she crawled along the form toward the seep of cool air and poked her head out of the bolt-hole.

The strong odor of her buck's chin-scent wafted to her from the bay willow screening the hole. Overhead, wings curried the breeze, and slender yellow catkins shuddered in the stir of wind. A tawny owl flurried to its nest in a rotting larch and shrieked hungrily, "ku-vv-itt," a signal to the waking kestrel that soon, with first light, the rite of hawking would pass to him.

Backing down the narrow stop, the doe slid into the nest chamber. The four kittens kindled the week before were awake, churning about in their sink in the ground, shredding the cover she had drawn over them.

The beginnings of a nap of fine fur powdered their nakedness. Splinters of teeth and claws showed. Although they had doubled in weight since birth, the ears that would loom large later bulged smaller than mushrooms. The kittens heard the doe enter, and groped blindly for her teats as she crouched over the shallow scoop.

Hungrily, they drew at her nipples, scrambling from one to the other, until she felt all eight raw and dry. Rising, she nuzzled the kittens into the bottom of the pocket.

The doe crawled to her stop and mixed the shags of fur from her belly with the grass. When she finished the pad, she returned to the nest chamber, tugging the blanket with her jaws.

The kittens were snugged in sleep. The doe licked the litter clean of their scattered pellets of feces and drew the pad over them.

Far off, a mole cricket shrilled, and closer, a wood warbler mimicked the cricket's whistle.

Turning her white scut toward the entrance, the doe gathered her soil loose in the burrow beneath her. Slowly she backed up, and at the opening her hind legs hurled out and scattered the dirt in the grass.

Outside, the doe ripped up and spread fresh birch-wort over the entrance. Suddenly she froze, as a harrier, riding an up-draft, threw a shadow in the faint light filtering through the brush.

The harrier soared and plunged, and drifted off.

The doe waited.

A woodpecker interrupted his drumming to call "kik!" Musk from a roe deer hovered in the air. A mole squeaked and blundered by, forelegs touching ground twice as often as hind.

At last, unable to detect untimely movement, the

doe sowed another cluster of leaves over the secured entrance and left.

Forepaws close together and hind feet apart, she hopped to the shelter of a hornbeam she had been girdling.

At the base of the trunk the doe rolled about in a spread of dust. Rising, she shook herself once, then combed her fur, using the long claws of her hind paws. Coating her pads with saliva, she pulled down and brushed each ear in turn. After extending her hind legs and feet to lick them clean, she sat for a moment in the sun. She vented, then turned to collect the pellets and chewed in a lazy sideward motion. The breeze freshened and rumpled her coat, and she moved head into wind, her fur now shedding the gust, her eyes closed but her nostrils winking for scent.

Her cud swallowed, the doe sucked up a lick of gravel, picked at a spray of sedge, and placed her forepaws on the trunk of the hornbeam. Cropping the bark, she widened the bare band she had gnawed at the base of the tree.

At the edge of the doe's vision, white flared. She turned. On the bough of a beech interlocking leaves with the hornbeam a stoat swayed. The doe watched as the stoat, no larger than two of her kittens, weaved its long slender neck back and forth—spooring, tracking. Slowly, the stoat's tail lifted and stiffened. The eyes riveted. The doe swung her head, and as she saw her buck standing in a tangle of knotgrass the stoat leaped.

From his dead stand, the buck burst out of the grass at full speed.

The stoat picked up the scent and scampered around the tangle of undergrowth, its body low to the ground.

The buck quartered; the stoat twisted. Hopping high, the buck glanced back at his pursuer and bounded over the fallen trunk of a mimosa. The stoat, gaining, scurried underneath.

As the stoat broke from the mimosa, the hare cut sharply, circling back. The stoat overran the buck's trail, veered, barked in anger.

On the far side of the hornbeam, the buck, bounding past his doe, swept through a patch of low meadow grass. The stoat cut his circle and hit.

Riding the hare's back, the stoat wrapped the buck's throat in his forelegs. The hare screamed in fear and shook, the sudden spasm tossing the stoat.

Free, the buck vaulted to the brow of a knoll and turned. His paw slapped the ground once, the thump ringing through the forest.

The stoat hurtled up the raise. The buck grunted, wheeled, and lashed out with his hind legs. The left flogged air but the claws of his right split the stoat's belly.

The stoat sprawled on the hare's withers, plunging his teeth into the buck's crest. Again the buck shrilled. Blood bubbled between the stoat's crunching jaws, but then his stomach broke loose and he slid from the hare's rump. The buck quivered, the stoat's teeth slacked, and the stoat pitched to the ground.

At the base of the hornbeam, the doe pushed away from the trunk and dropped to her forepaws.

She faced her buck. A stump of cloud dragged its shadow across the clearing. Behind the buck a firecrest called thinly. Over the dead stoat flies surged, and through the swarm a kestrel dropped to pick at the carcass.

A buzzard coasted overhead once, turned, and fluttered low across the field. The kestrel fled. The buzzard lit and perched on the stoat's stifle.

The doe's scut snapped up. She thumped her hind foot in warning. The buck continued to hunker, unmoving.

The doe's hind foot drummed again as the second buzzard swept in, skimming over the buck, its claws brushing his fur. The buzzard soared and hooked in a turn. The buck rose. Darting down the knoll, he found cover in a hassock of sorrel.

The buck sat, his ears moving to trap sound. Assured, he jumped in the air and came down facing the doe. Frisking, he started toward her.

At the edge of the sorrel, the stoat's mate struck.

The stoat drove for the jugular. Her long canine teeth bit and ripped and tore, her jaws throbbing as quickly as hummingbird wings—draining blood before the buck's head toppled to the ground.

The stoat drank but did not feed. She circled the buck and snagged his haunch. Dragging the hare, she cleared the sorrel.

Suddenly—dropping the buck, she bolted.

The doe heard the stoat flutter through the scrub. The stoat swept past her, and before she could move the stoat had seized the first of the kittens and snapped its neck.

Tumbling—spilling blindly over each other—the litter slid along the roots of the birchwort.

The doe shot forward. The stoat bit off the head of the second kitten and had turned to the third when the driving doe slammed her off balance. Whirling, the stoat snapped; the doe shied. As the stoat whipped back to the third kitten, she was rocked off balance by the doe's kick. Spinning, the stoat leaped across the doe's back, slicing off her ear. The doe squealed in pain but lashed out with her hind legs, missing—kicking again—then heeling about.

The stoat was gone; with her, the last kitten.

The doe hunched a moment, her one ear tacking, straining for a ripple from the stoat.

The odd lull in the forest turned the doe toward her stop. A whir passed over and skimmed through the scrub. Her nose twitching, the doe cowered, then broke for the burrow's entrance. As she flung forward, the second arrow struck, splitting through her shoulder to the heart.

Dry brush cracked under light steps.

Two boys stood over the doe. The younger, Perchik, shifted the bow to his left hand, grasped the shaft at the crest, and withdrew it.

The elder bent down—his light, flax hair pitching over his eyes—and lifted the doe by its hind legs. From Ritter's other hand two hares dangled.

"The weasel got her ear."

"Who eats the ear?"

"Hoegel's fussy."

"I'm not—"

Ritter fidgeted and tossed back the fall of hair. "There you go again. If Hoegel finds we're eating his kill—"

Perchik laughed and slid the arrow into a birch-bark quiver slung over his shoulder.

"Asshead . . . we'll bury the bones."

2

THE MOVEMENT FADED. The needle rasped on the record turning in the old Aeolian-Vocalion, and then the slow section began. The tall man stretched lazily on the padded table opposite the solid oak Gothic bed and rolled to his back, covering his groin with the perfumed hand towel.

He opened his eyes and said, "The French chalk, Stepan."

His loose leather sandals clumping, the boy crossed to the wood shelf, returned with the container, and spread the powder on his palms. Cupping the man's right heel in his left hand, he kneaded the large toe.

"Stroke, Stepan."

Stepan caressed Hoegel's instep with his fingers and thumb.

"Like this, Commandant?"

"Hmn-n."

Commandant Hoegel shut his eyes. The muted strings joined the variation.

"Stepan . . . diminuendo—"

Stepan nodded to Ritter, standing in the corner of the whitewashed room. Moving to the inlaid-mahogany phonograph, Ritter passed the two dead hares from his left to his right hand, and twisted his fingers counterclockwise, without touching the knob. Stepan nodded. Ritter bent—the shock of sandy hair capsizing to his eyes—and lowered the volume.

"Bravo, Reger, bravo." The Commandant breathed deeply in appreciation and contentment. "Brash. Bolder than Brahms. Absolutely reckless. Even Brahms wouldn't choose A major as an element in a work in G."

Stepan released the pressure of his thumbs on the Commandant's kneecap and said, "No, sir."

The Commandant said, "Was that you, Stepan?"

Stepan cocked his head to the side to look at the Commandant with his clear eye; the other, along with the cheekbone, was missing. His skin was fair, the chaff on his shaved head fine, his lips thin but with form. One half his face was graceful, the other half— the buckle under his eye drawing up the tip of the mouth—deformed.

"Yes, sir."

Fear left Stepan with the Commandant's chuckle. "You agree?"

"With what you said, sir—"

"Reger has experimented interestingly?"

"He must have."

Still smiling, the Commandant held up his right arm. Stepan moved to Hoegel's side and slapped his forearm energetically with a cupped palm.

The Commandant fell in with the reprise, humming two bars, then said, "And you?"

The talc curled like smoke. Ritter sneezed. "Me, sir?"

"Stepan, are we alone?"

"No, sir."

Ritter brushed his wrist across his nose. "I don't know."

"What don't you know, Ritter?"

"About this composer, sir."

"That's honest. Are you honest, Stepan?"

"I try, sir."

"Tell me more about Reger's impudence."

"Who's Reger, sir?"

"That's better, Stepan."

Stepan tapped his fingers up the Commandant's biceps to his shoulder, then hacked the muscles briskly with the heel of his hand.

Hoegel said, "Only a church organist would dare obliterate the cadence—"

The orchestra plunged into a dark B flat, lost the original tempo, and returned to the home tonic.

"Splendid."

The movement ended. The needle fretted in the empty groove. Beneath the single window with the drawn curtain, a large dog growled. A fly seethed in and out of the French chalk hanging like mist, returning again and again to the two carcasses dangling from Ritter's hand.

"Shall I turn the record over, Commandant?"

"Later—"

Stepan pointed with his shoulder. Ritter stepped to the Aeolian-Vocalion, shut off the turntable, closed the polished lid, and replaced the decanter lamp that Stepan had made for the Commandant from a fiasco of Italian wine.

The fly sputtered. Stepan moved to the Commandant's left side. Hoegel said softly, "—when we finish."

Holding the Commandant's fingers, Stepan stroked Hoegel's left hand from the wrist to the elbow.

"Will I eat well this evening, Stepan?"

"Yes, sir."

"Are the hares both female?"

"Both male, sir."

"You're sure?"

"Yes, Commandant."

"Plump?"

"One—" Stepan circled the Commandant's arm, pressed, moved the bracelet of fingers up a few millimeters, pressed again. "The second is sick."

The Commandant laughed. "Sick? Are you a vet, Stepan?"

Stepan looked to Ritter, who said, "No, sir, but we found things."

"What things?"

"Flukes. Worms, too, and the liver was white."

"Shouldn't it be?"

"No, sir. Also, the fur's full of ticks and fleas."

"Did you shoot your way into a rabbit funeral?"

"No, Commandant. You ordered me to bring in everything I trap."

"That's true, Ritter. And the other?"

"The other's young."

"How young?"

"Not a year."

The fly fishtailed to the Commandant's chest and Stepan puffed it off.

"Can you tell a rabbit's age? Thank you, Stepan."

"Not always, but this one's about ten months—"

"Did he carry papers?"

"No, sir, but the bones of his legs were beginning to harden."

"Ah—" The Commandant blew dust from his nostrils. "Should I know that?"

Ritter's furrowed eyebrows begged Stepan for a lead.

"Does everyone out there?"

Stepan motioned to Ritter to answer, but Ritter shrugged.

"Who shut off the phonograph?"

Stepan said, "You asked us to. Do you wish to hear the other side?"

"Start over."

Ritter moved the decanter lamp, lifted the lid, placed the needle, and clicked the knob. The opening phrases of the Orchestral Serenade, Opus 95, washed across the room.

"You, Ritter—"

"Yes, Commandant?"

"Do you have everything you need? Bait?"

"Yes, sir."

"Traps?"

"One is broken."

"I'll send a mechanic with you."

"Oh, no. I'll bring it in." The hares were beginning to feel heavy. Ritter shifted his grip to the foreshanks, shaking the fly loose.

Hoegel said, "Young man—"

"Yes, sir?"

"You're not hiding a lover out there—"

"No, sir. I'm alone. I've never seen anyone. Especially a woman."

"Especially—"

Reaching down, Hoegel straightened the edge of the perfumed towel.

"Ritter."

"Commandant?"

The fly sizzled over the hare's flank.

"The proper word is naturally."

"Sir?"

"Leave the rabbits. Take the fly with you."

Ritter whacked the hare's rib, but the fly buzzed away.

Moving to the Commandant's leg, Stepan cupped Hoegel's left heel, kneading the toe.

"Would you like to join me for dinner?"

The fly set on the scut. Ritter moved to the door, treading carefully.

Stepan said, "Yes. Oh, yes, sir." He did not finish molding the toe. Lowering the Commandant's leg to the table, Stepan crossed to the wood shelf. He replaced the French talc and wiped his hands on his hopsack trousers. Removing a jar of aromatic cocoa butter, he stirred in fresh oil of bergamot. Stepan returned to the table and spread the lubricant over the Commandant's abdomen. Plucking up the sleeves of his coarse wool shirt, both hands stretched out flat, palms side by side, Stepan stroked Hoegel's stomach in small circles.

Ritter opened the door, stepped into the volley of sunlight, and called, "Stepan!"

Ritter heard only the sweep of a harp.

"Stepan!"

The door opened wider. Stepan had slipped off his

leather sandals. Ritter shook loose the fly and handed the hares to Stepan. The door rammed shut.

Ritter heard the hares thump to the floor and the bolt yoke.

Shielding and closing his eyes, Ritter bounced down the steps of the pergola. Before the glare eased, he heard the slop-slop. Squinting, he saw three women in front of him, on hands and knees, whitewashing the large boulders along the gravel path leading to the Commandant's caserne. All wore the same short gray uniform, and their underthings were frayed and torn. Pink showed through, and on one—

The blow to the ear knocked Ritter to his knees. He rolled over. The guard looking down said nothing.

Ritter pushed himself backward. The guard grinned. Ritter rose running.

3

THE RUMBLE woke Ritter. He listened, but Perchik, breathing evenly, did not stir.

"Twenty," Ritter said, and began to count. At "nineteen" the wash of rain billowed over the crawl-hole.

Ritter closed his eyes. Their pit was well sealed. His eyes drew as little light open as closed.

The rain would be heavy and steady, and last the night. There'd be some seepage from the dirt walls, and the wood slabs they slept on would turn dank. The logs, brush, and canvas plugging the crawl-hole had held always, but they'd never worked out a way to push open their bung after a storm without runoff.

Paws crumped heavily in deadwood. A boar—rooting and stalking—snorted hungrily. Ritter hoped for another bolt to rouse Perchik, but the rain drummed monotonously, lashed into an occasional spasm by the wind.

"Yerik!"

Perchik tossed on his wood slab, and Ritter was about to ask whether he had ever heard a frog this far from the wallow, but Perchik's gentle wheeze never wavered and Ritter sifted the puzzle in silence.

"Yer-rr-rik—"

Ritter slapped the floor, but the frog had romped away.

The frog must have slipped in during the daylight airing.

Since the two invasions, they kept their dirt socket as clean as their traps. When first they'd dug the pit, they'd hidden their food as well as themselves—and drawn mice; and once the Commandant had pressed a straw mattress on Ritter and only a fire had rid them of the cockroaches.

"Yerr-r . . . yerik!"

Ritter hitched to his elbow.

"Perchik."

"Um-m."

"Perchik!"

"M-m-m."

Ritter reached over in the dark, found Perchik's nostrils, and pinched. "Wake up."

"Ritter, please—"

Ritter released Perchik's nose. "There's a frog."

"Where's a frog?"

The croak was smothered: "yherrk—"

"Under you—"

"Go to sleep, Ritter. He's outside."

"Perchik . . . please, Perchik, listen."

Ritter tracked sound: water riffled; a grasshopper chirped; Perchik wheezed.

Ritter rolled over and pressed his arm into his ear. Through the night he had dreamed of sleeping, but each time he drowsed the frog croaked. Once, on waking, Ritter listened to a spittle bug's tireless whistle; later, he heard a squirrel ranging in the shrub, fleeing with a frightened squeal from a silent stalker. As the night dragged along, the air in the hollow grew heavy with their breath, and in the dampness Ritter felt as if he were drowning. A "yerik" throbbed; a muffled grumble far away told him the storm had drifted off, drawing the cloudburst with it.

"Perchik."

"Um-m?"

"Is it morning?"

"Not yet."

"How soon?"

"Soon."

"A half-hour?"

"Maybe less."

"Are you up?"

"I'm up."

"How could you sleep with the frog?"

"Frog?"

"Perchik—"

"What?"

"After I kill him, I'm finishing finishing finishing you."

"Me? When?"

"When it's light."

"Then I have a half-hour?"

"If I let you live that long."

Through his front teeth Perchik whistled a chorus of "Three Blind Mice," then: "Ritter—"

"Yes?"

"Why didn't you use the flashlight?"

Ritter dropped from his slab to the dirt floor. "The light! Where did we hide it?"

"We hid it for an emergency."

"Where?"

"We agreed only to show light—"

Ritter fumbled in the dark for Perchik's ankle. "Per-chik."

"—if you got lost."

Ritter tightened his grip. "Where is it?"

"In a hole under my boards."

Ritter groped along Perchik's body. Perchik said, "The batteries must be dead."

Ritter pinned Perchik's shoulders. Perchik tumbled to the floor, set his right foot on the dirt shelf holding Ritter's bed and pushed through the canvas plugging the crawl-hole, showering Ritter.

Feet straddling the wet sod on both sides of the opening, Perchik leaned in and said, "Hah!"

In his hand he held the flashlight.

Ritter stepped into his hobnailed boots and scrambled out. Still sweating from the pit, he shivered in the brisk night air. Water lost its grip on the overhanging box elder and dripped icy needles to his neck. His breath hung on his lips, a balloon of dew. The sky was murky, but early light, groping for tree tips, threw shadows. He could not see Perchik, but then a covey of lapwings boiled up to his right. Ritter started forward and Perchik broke with a laugh from a hedge of barberry.

At first Ritter heard only the brush of Perchik's plunge through the wood—the whisk past a runner of silverweed, the raking of blackthorn.

Ritter followed. Squeaking, voles skittered out of his way. Mud under night-damp sucked at his feet. A magpie scolded.

Running, Ritter shied under an overhang of mistletoe and in the clearing ahead saw a swift shadow sweep into the brook. He lengthened his stride.

Perchik turned to measure his lead and skidded on a patch of moss in the water. Ritter dived from the bank—soaring with arms stretched—splashing flat on his stomach as Perchik spun.

Ritter's fingers closed on a hank of hair. Both sank to the shallow bottom and bobbed up spluttering. Perchik slipped free but Ritter leaped again, hooking Perchik's shin. Perchik tumbled to the far bank. Ritter squirmed forward and slipped his arm around Perchik's waist.

Perchik rolled to his back and started to laugh. Ritter straddled Perchik, sitting on his chest, the shag of wet hair masking his eyes. Perchik tore loose his right hand and pointed the flashlight at Ritter. His finger clicked the switch.

"Dead—"

"I don't want the flashlight. I want you."

Ritter twisted the light from Perchik's hand, threw it into the grass, and shifted his grip to Perchik's throat.

Perchik was still grinning. "Why?"

"You let the frog get away."

"He didn't get away."

"You let him out."

"The frog didn't get away."

Perchik puffed his cheeks, puckered his lips, and croaked: "Yer-*rik!*"

Digging his heels into the soft ground, Perchik slid down, through Ritter's fingers and between his legs.

Ritter remained on his knees. Perchik crept up behind and grumbled softly: "Yer . . . yer-r-ik."

Ritter turned, his face rigid.

"You . . you weren't sleeping!"

"I'm not running any more."

"Perchik—"

"I'm not. Don't start again. I'll fight."

"Perchik . . . teach me."

4

RITTER shook loose the beads of water and draped the canvas used to cover the crawl-hole over Perchik's wood slab, facing the single slant of sun. Squirming through the narrow entrance, he stood at the edge of the pit, blinking in the strong morning light.

The smell of the fire brought a burble of hunger from his stomach. Kneeling, Ritter peered under the rock slab covering the trench stove. The fuzz sticks had fired the kindling. He slid the split fat pine over the flames and stepped back. An eddy of smoke straggled to the woven screen of larch boughs propped on four holly sticks over the stove. The screen broke apart the trail of smudge, scattering the smoke. Perchik was still at the stream; Ritter moved the empty pot to the side of the slab.

Ritter bent over the crawl-hole, arranged the boughs of ash to conceal the opening, and shinnied up the locust tree to the cache. Reaching under the conical shield hanging flare-end down to keep out mice, Ritter withdrew two roasted thighs from the birch basket and four sugar cubes—and retucked the netting. As he slid down the trunk, Ritter saw the bob of Perchik's cinnamon hair along the slope of the bank.

Ritter dropped the cubes into the pot, placed the

roast hare on the slab, and had picked a full fist of elderberry when he heard the faint clank.

Gripping two steel traps at the baseplate—a canteen slung over his shoulder—Perchik pushed to the edge of the small clearing behind Ritter. Shorter than Ritter—slighter—Perchik stopped a moment before stepping from the cover of the forest, then crossed silently and laid the traps along the wall of the trench stove. Ritter held out his fist; Perchik opened his hand and Ritter dropped in half the elderberries. Perchik nodded, popped the fruit into his mouth, and unslung the strap of the canteen.

The warm pot with the sugar cubes hissed when Ritter poured in the water. He asked, "What held you up?"

Perchik removed the flashlight from his pocket.

"You threw it under deadwood."

"Who would see it there?"

"Alsatians, Ritter von Ritterhof. They sniff things out."

Ritter shrugged. "You outsniff any dog of Hoegel's."

Using the two ends of a green pole bent double, Ritter turned over the thighs. With the ends of his tongs he jabbed at the fire. Perchik sat on his heels.

The flames fluttered. Softly, the fat pine popped. Wind shifted the smoke; Ritter waved the smudge toward the larch screen.

Ritter brushed back his hair and said, "I don't know about Hoegel."

"He's been good to you."

"Rausch was good."

Perchik said, "Rausch was good and didn't do anything."

Ritter tried to sound hopeful. "Maybe Hoegel meant it, but hasn't had time."

"They both had time, if they wanted to."

Ritter drew one of the gin traps along the ground and examined it for blood and fur. Perchik said, "It's washed clean. I tried to fix it, but the broken spring's coming loose."

Ritter said, "I told Hoegel. He wants to send a mechanic."

Alarmed, Perchik flared, "Ritter!"

Calming him, Ritter said, "I'll bring it in."

Ritter propped the gin against the sod side of the stove. "He sure loves hare. More than Rausch. He keeps bringing it up, but grown people—"

Ritter unsheathed his Solingen knife and tested the shank with the nib of the blade. "When grown people say something, sometimes you know they don't mean it, right from the beginning." Ritter turned the meat. "But even those that mean it—forget . . ."

"Everyone knows that. Grown people don't even tell each other the truth."

Ritter lifted one of the thighs and swung it toward Perchik. The bite into the flesh sluiced fat over Perchik's chin. Carefully, he licked the run into his mouth. Ritter closed his eyes and rubbed his nose on the bone of the second thigh, snorting gustily.

His mouth clotted with meat and juices, Ritter said, "Was Hoegel straight about my uncle?"

"As much as grown people can be."

"You don't believe him—"

"I didn't see . . . I can usually tell, Ritter, when I look at them."

Ritter licked at the joint and then sucked his fingers.

"When they came for my uncle, they said he'd be back for dinner."

"Uniforms?"

"They were very polite."

Perchik tapped out marrow. "Uniforms are the worst."

"They even asked him to sign his name in one of his books. The soldier with stripes on his sleeves had a silver pen."

"Books are trouble—"

"What's wrong with you, Perchik? Everything's trouble. Books. Uniforms. Grown people."

Perchik looked into Ritter's blue eyes. "Ritter," he said gloomily, "books mean your uncle was a Socialist."

"What's a Socialist?"

"Socialists are bad."

"Why?"

"I don't know why. But I heard they're bad. They were bad first, before anyone else."

Perchik tossed the stripped bone under the slab into the fire. In the reeds fringing the wallow, a waterrail squealed, and nearby a crossbill ripped through a cone scale to its seeds.

Perchik said, "My parents had a friend who was a Socialist. Over his fireplace he had a chart; his cousin way back on his mother's side was Frederick the Second. When the uniforms came, he showed them a lock of the Emperor's hair in a safe behind the chart. They kept the hair and whipped him with a cane."

Perchik churned the water in the pot with his finger, melting the sugar cubes. He took the tongs from Ritter, and turning them about, thrust the curved end into the fire and tightened it over a small hot rock. He dropped the rock into the pot, removed a collapsible metal cup from his pocket, and poured in the simmering, sweet drink. Ritter held out his cup and said, "Hoegel will find my uncle."

Perchik moved into a spill of sun and faced up. His tan had darkened to cocoa.

"Your uncle's dead."

"You think so, Perchik?"

"Everyone's dead."

"We're not dead."

"Sooner or later they'll get tired of you and find me."

"Please, Perchik—" Ritter's cheeks paled. "How soon, Perchik?"

"Oh, we have time. We'll reach twenty-five, even thirty—"

Ritter looked relieved. Teasing, Perchik said, "—between us."

Now Ritter laughed and swung at Perchik's ear. Perchik rolled away and came to his feet without spilling a drop. Draining his cup, Perchik said, "Let's clean up and I'll race you to the water."

"First we have to set the traps."

"Oh, the Commandant says . . . line them up straight."

Ritter's tone changed. "Don't start that again."

"Bring everything in to Poppa Hoegel—"

Ritter shoveled a handful of leaves toward Perchik, who romped clear of the shower of dirt, lilting with a singsong "Poppa will give you your share—"

Ritter turned away and nuzzled his cup.

"And you kiss the Commandant's iddy—"

Wheeling, Ritter shot forward, reaching out and dropping flat to his chest. Perchik fell back, but Ritter held his ankle. Ritter said, "You'll roast fine, just fine. Not much fat, but juicy, juicy—"

Perchik kicked at Ritter's wrist with his free foot. Ritter tightened his grip and squirmed closer.

A long whistle reeled through the trees.

Ritter released Perchik and jumped to his feet. "Maybe this time there'll be fruit."

Again, the train shrilled.

Ritter started to run. Perchik seized the tongs, knelt in front of the trench stove—banking the fire—and called, "Ritter!"

At the edge of the clearing Ritter stopped.

His voice slack, Perchik said softly, "If you can't remember—I can't stay."

In the distance, steam brewed up.

Impatiently, Ritter muttered, "Oh, Perchik," and crossed to the locust tree, lifting a square of turf from high ground at its base. He gathered the two metal cups, the pot, and the flashlight. Kneeling beside the opening under the sod, Ritter tucked the equipment into the hole against the wall of plaited brush and dried strops of rabbit hide. Carefully, he replaced the turf.

Perchik had struck two of the holly sticks; Ritter plucked up the other pair. Perchik laid his sticks and the wood tongs over the slab. Ritter dropped his poles on top. Together they lowered the woven screen of larch boughs.

Ritter stepped back. Perchik scattered brush along the edge of the screen, breaking the straight line.

Ritter grinned. "Feel safe now?"

Perchik stepped to Ritter's side, probing: had they covered their traces?

From the train, steel crumped, coupling a car.

Perchik said, "There's still smoke—"

Ritter squeezed a jeer through his nostrils and ran. For a moment Perchik studied the web of smoke, thinning as it rose; then he turned. He passed Ritter as they splashed across the stream.

5

"THEIRS is much lower than ours."

Ritter wriggled forward to the edge of the ridge and spread the slender stalks of bindweed.

In the pocket below, the Lithuanian prisoner in gray bent over, mixing fresh paint. The young sergeant in a uniform one size too large—his cloth cap drooped to the bridge of his nose—waited. Sitting on a leather-covered shooting stick, the lieutenant bawled a command Ritter could not hear.

The prisoner Antanas snapped up the stencil and bucket and hurried toward the young girl at the head of the last line.

Lying on his back, Perchik picked lazily at a dung-fly bite, leaving light scratch marks on his tanned cheek. "It's not in front?"

"No. I hear the slit's way down."

"Near the other hole?"

"That's why they have to sit, even when they pee."

"What's the hair for?"

"I once asked Paulder. He whopped me on the ear and shouted, 'Dummy, it's the world's most effective decoration.'"

"What does 'effective' mean?"

"I was afraid to ask."

Ritter fetched a wild cherry from his pocket and tucked it into his cheek. "I like it full."

The train beside the platform released air from its brakes. Smoke from the engine drifted over the cars behind—the first open, the next two shut—and into the fresh morning sky. The sun cleared the eastern hogback straddling the notch, and from the hills sloping to the railroad bed daybreak's dew steamed.

Perchik snickered. "Me, too."

Antanas, followed by the sergeant in billowing trousers, walked along the row of women, painting a red roll number on each arm, occasionally kicking away a torn valise held together with rope or strips of blanket.

Spitting out the stem, Ritter said, "Growing like weeds—"

"Dark." Perchik giggled. "So you can really see."

"The one the Lithuanian's painting—you'll see, she's thick."

"How can you tell?"

"She's so round on top."

Perchik rolled over and squirmed to the edge of the bluff. Spreading the slender stalks where they joined in the middle, he peeped through a cluster of small white flowers.

The lieutenant rose, moved to the side for a clear view of the woman with her left arm outstretched, and tugged the flared edge of his custom black uniform through the belt high on his waist, dipping slightly at the knees to relieve the pressure of his crotch-hugging plus fours.

Perchik said, "You can't tell. I bet sometimes they're big on top with nothing on bottom."

"So far, her top's the best." Ritter sucked on the cherry pit. "Except for that one to the right, near the end. She looks like she's clogged up."

"Everyone made jokes."

"You know her?"

Perchik nodded.

"From your town?"

"The skinny one beside her, too. Cousins. The big one's Emma Peller."

"Emma?"

"Emma."

Ritter sang, "Her name . . . is . . . Emma . . . Peller—"

Perchik looked at Ritter, who dug his elbow into Perchik's shoulder and winked. "You liked her."

"Oh, she's old. She's fifteen."

"You just peeked from far—"

"Ritter—"

"The lieutenant likes her, too. He's telling the sergeant he wants her." Ritter kicked Perchik with his foot. "Why don't we join the army?"

Perchik rolled to his back. The sun made him close his eyes, but then shadow eased the glare. Perchik studied the drift of cloud. With wide wings, it could be a stork; or, with a tail, an otter.

Ritter said, "He's in a rush to finish now."

The cloud curled. An otter. No—the tail was too short. A young polecat.

"Emma's so big she's floppy."

The cat gathered to spring.

"The sister's nothing."

"Cousin."

"Not a thing. Looks like a boy with a piece missing."

Below, a truck turned over its engine and fired.

Ritter said, "There's one suitcase on the platform. She left it behind."

"Who?"

"Emma."

"Dumb Emma . . . you think she left it to pick up on the way home tonight?"

Gears ground as the truck started up the dirt road. A heavy door slid along steel runners and clanked open.

"Here come the men." Ritter cracked the cherry pit and sprayed flakes. "There's one in a bowler. Must be the banker."

Perchik heard shouts and thumps, and the darting and scuffling of feet. Ritter turned to Perchik. "The last car also looks like men. No supplies on this train. Should we go?"

The cat sprang, freeing the sun to blaze out of a clear sky. Perchik said, "I could sleep."

Ritter pried open a blade of the Solingen and picked his teeth.

Along the wooden platform, men and boys were being formed into four rows of ten by the sergeant in the uniform one size too large. There were more children than usual; dark-haired, light-boned, frightened. One boy, at the far end, looked different. His shock of hair was red almost, as if dusted with cinnamon.

Ritter said, "Do you have a twin?"

Perchik shut his eyes against the sun. The afterglow burned out slowly. Rolling to his stomach, he pushed forward on his elbows into the bindweed.

Ritter said, "At the back. He stands out. The funniest-looking one in the load."

Perchik squinted through the screen of white flowers, then dropped his head to the ground.

Ritter said lightly, "Don't faint. He's uglier than a hedgehog—"

But then Perchik turned toward him, and Ritter read Perchik's face, and was frightened.

6

THE GUARD had seen him often in the compound —arriving with trussed hares, lugging away traps and chains and stake pins. Today the youngster with the hair like ripe flax did not turn toward the Commandant's caserne, but hurried down a side path. The guard passed on, his heavy boots crunching in the gravel. If he were Hoegel, the guard thought, he would let his poacher of fresh game run wild—if he wanted to—in a Russian tank.

Ritter followed the narrow path and stopped in front of the small barrack backed against the barbed-wire fence.

Ritter's second knock raised a stir behind the wooden door, but no response.

"I can hear you in there," he said.

The words from inside were more breath than sound. "Go away."

"Open the door."

"No one's allowed."

"Please."

"What do you want?"

"Help."

"From me?"

"Open!"

After a long pause, Stepan answered. "Wait."

Ritter heard him move away from the door. Curtains slid along rods, and then a dead bolt snapped. Stepan peeped out, squinting down at Ritter. Stepan released the stub, and the chain guard holding the door fell free.

Ritter stepped inside. Behind him, Stepan bolted the door and ran the stub back into its fluting.

The room was dark. Ritter smelled wood shavings and metal and neat's-foot oil. Gradually his eyes adjusted. Stepan's bed stood in a corner, a patchwork of stitched rabbit pelts his blanket. The back seat of an old Maybach sedan served as a couch, covered by hides cinched together with goatskin laces. Out of stacked train wheels, shimmering under grease, a lamp had been fashioned, its shade a drum of embossed leather. On a butcher's block converted to a workbench, a length of black pine was clamped in a vise, its end half chamfered. A single slash of light fell across the calcimined wall. On a large calendar tacked over the head of the bed, a girl gave herself to the sun on a French beach. Behind the closed curtains the windows were shut, and in the stale air Stepan's sweat hung heavily.

Stepan did not leave the door. "What do you want?"

Ritter turned. "Why are you looking at me like that?"

"I told you, the Commandant doesn't allow anyone to come here."

"I'm your friend, Stepan."

"Hoegel says I shouldn't have friends. I'm not supposed to be alone with anyone. I'm supposed to stay locked in this room, until he sends for me."

Stepan crossed to the butcher's block, picked up the

jack plane, and set it down again. "I can't ask Hoegel for anything."

"Hoegel mustn't find out about this," Ritter said.

"He wouldn't be happy?"

"Happy? No."

"Would it hurt him?"

"Well . . . he'd be angry."

Stepan crossed to his bed. Nervously, he plucked at the nap of rabbit fur. "One of the corporals saw me looking at a woman prisoner."

"Did you?"

"I only looked."

"All people look."

"I'm always careful. I hide and the women don't know."

"Did the corporal report you to Hoegel?" Ritter asked.

"He said he might. He said Hoegel would beat me. He said he might not tell Hoegel, but I had to think of him."

"I don't understand."

"He said he would like to play with me, like the Commandant." Outside the patrol passed on the far side of the fence. "Hoegel said what we do would be between us. A secret. No one would ever find out." Stepan's voice chipped. "If the corporal knows, everyone knows."

"What does Hoegel do to you?"

Stepan jerked out a hank of fur.

"You don't like it, do you?"

Stepan shook his head. Ritter sat on the cowhide couch and whispered, "Then find David Fehrmann."

Ritter wasn't sure Stepan had heard; then a faint murmur filtered out of the darkness. "Who's David Fehrmann?"

"He's in one of the work barracks."

"I need his number."

"I don't have it."

"How do I find him? No one has a name here."

"I can tell you what he looks like."

"They're jammed in like rabbits. Can you tell one rabbit from another?"

"Stepan, listen. *Please*. He's younger than me, almost ten, very thin. Dark, but not as dark as Gypsies. Brown eyes. Funny hair, like your lampshade, only redder."

"Why is he important?"

"It's better you don't know," Ritter said.

"Finding Fehrmann hurts Hoegel, doesn't it?" Stepan turned his clear eye to Ritter and smiled.

7

PERCHIK shivered.

He'd thought awake he'd keep a closer measure of time than asleep, but he had no idea whether the night was half over, close to dawn, or far short of midnight. There had been no rain, but earlier, water had begun to ooze from the ground. Dew soaked the burlap covering his tennis shoes, filling the pocket in front of his toes with water, where the sneakers were too large. The gray pair of prison trousers he'd drawn over the worn lederhosen Ritter had stolen from the compound were damp, and his thin cotton shirt clung soggily to his chest and back.

Nearby, a frog grunted in the wallow. Perchik closed his eyes and thought of their pit, and for a moment felt not the tall ash but the wood slab against his back—and tasted air stale with Ritter's sweat.

A rustle opened Perchik's eyes. He tilted his head. The sweep of sound was high, not in the brush. In a gathering rush, a dead tree tore loose its withered roots and plunged, hitting hard and setting off a clamor of shrieks and screeches.

Pushing away from the trunk of the ash, Perchik leaned on the stave of the yew bow and rose stiffly from his squat. He swayed, dazed, as if his sudden rise had drained his head of blood. He leaned his left hand against the rutted bark. Grumbling in the dark, he cursed the cold, the wetness, the sun for not coming up, the deer for their cunning.

Perchik wiped a wad of mud from the point and dropped his arrow into the birchbark quiver. He tossed the sinew sling over his shoulder and stepped around a knot of yellow and green mousetail.

Perhaps the deer track on the bank of the stream were older than he'd thought. Or perhaps this night the deer were at the still water downstream, or had clustered at the salt lick on the choked point punching into the wallow.

Perchik moved carefully in the dark, but after he had taken only a few steps a jagged leaf of thorn apple hooked into his trousers. Gripping the oval leaf at its point, he worked the poisonous spine free.

He stood a moment. The wind was lively, laced with the sting of resin. A redstart warbled, ending its burst with a perky twitter. To his left, phosphorescent wood flared. In spite of everything Perchik felt like singing. Was it wrong? Who would hear? Who would know? Momma and Poppa were dead, Ritter slept in the pit, the prison camp sat at the far end of the wood.

No one would hear, except Perchik, of course. Perchik would know—know that he'd been singing, singing because he was free, singing—might it be—because he was not Dudie . . .

He chilled at the thought of his brother, rubbed his free hand briskly against the arm holding the yew bow and stepped around an overhang of elm. He cut the trail to the wallow and trotted easily, the burlap sponging out water each time he set foot on the cover of leaves, until he reached the shallows facing the point.

Perchik sat on the bank, looking across at the spit of land. The point was choked with a thick growth of osier, the long green leaves showing silky white undersides each time they bobbed in the breeze.

Under a sky smoky with clouds, the wallow lay flat and dull, a lazy eddy near the inflow raising and dropping beds of arrowhead and red asphodel. A grebe whickered and drifted by—submerged to its head—rose slowly, and with a parting gabble surfaced and took to the air, the beat of its brown wings riffling the water underneath.

Perchik leaned against the trunk of a young mespil and slipped his right shoulder from the sinew string. He selected and drew an arrow from the quiver. Cradling the bow in his lap, he reached to the upper end of the yew stave and pushed the string forward into the notch. He nocked the arrow and dropped the bow into his left palm, the handgrip balanced and resting in his open fingers.

Perchik stared hard at the rippling white undersides of the osier. If their rhythm broke, it might be the passing of game . . . If they drifted to the lick, the game might be deer . . .

At first the sudden light seemed a storm flash . . . but he heard neither rain nor thunder. Then Perchik saw the glow lapping weakly over the sawtooth ridge of pine and fir and knew he had dozed.

He'd wasted another night. How many more would he have? How long could he keep failing Dudie?

Perchik tried to rise, but was cramped with cold. He clenched his fingers, set his fist into the hoarfrost on the ground, and pushed. Painfully his legs straightened.

Perchik slipped the arrow into the quiver, stamped the ice off the burlap, and turned into the brush.

He drifted along the path he and Ritter had worn to the wallow. His steps heavy, his toes numb in the icy sludge thick in the toes of his tennis shoes, Perchik hobbled to the shelf of the small creek.

The thin wash, black during the night, was now deep blue in the haze of morning. The stream ran swiftly, tumbling over boulders and shale along its uneven banks. Loosening and setting his quiver beside the bow, Perchik dropped to his knees. The ground was hard and cold, the water icy. He drank, then lowered his face. Plugging each ear with a forefinger, he dipped his head low. His scalp tingled with shock. Pulling up, he shook the water out of his hair—but he hadn't jammed his fingers tightly. Fluid swirled on his drum. He tipped his head, thumped the ear with his open palm, and felt warmed water trickle out.

Bending forward, Perchik stiffened his fingers like prongs and rubbed down his scalp.

The whir in his ear continued.

Perchik waggled his head. The hum swelled to a whistle—shrill, drawn-out, piping.

His fingers stopped, his body motionless, still as a stump.

The whistle was answered—downstream.

At a hook in the drop facing him, a wild lentil bloomed. As Perchik studied the yellow buds, the lentil moved—a jar, not the ruffle of a passing gust.

Slowly, his body rigid, Perchik reached behind with his left hand for the bow—and drew an arrow from the quiver.

Leaving his left knee on the ground, he lifted his right.

Should he sight low for a fawn, high for a doe, or over the crest of the lentil for a stag? Or should he close his eyes, and loose—for luck?

Feeling for the cock feather, Perchik slid the butt of the arrow to the nocking point, locked the first joint of his thumb over the string, and clamped the thumb between the first two fingers of his right hand.

Again he heard the drawn-out call from behind the bank of flowers, followed by a bleat upstream—shorter, pitched higher. A yearling answering its hind.

Perchik canted the bow and drew, anchoring high on the cheekbone. Holding the bow in his left hand—his fingers slack—he waited.

Over the jostling black pods of the lentil the dark muzzle of a roe deer showed, followed by the head. Her ears—cups to the side, a dark trace outlining the edges—fidgeted for sound.

Perchik loosed. The arrow arched and its pile struck the hind's gullet—low—the shaft sinking deep.

The dark muzzle took the arrow with it. Perchik plunged into the water, leaning into the raw stream, muttering at the sudden weight of the soaked burlap wrapping his feet.

On the far side of the lentil he found flecks on the flowers and streaks along the ground, and near the base of a sun spurge, clabbered blood. Perchik lowered his head and drove through a web of hop, and in the clearing behind, the arrow lay.

Perchik dropped to his knees and lifted the ash shaft. The hen feathers and the cock feather had not held in the fletching. The arrow had gone through.

Perchik trembled, but couldn't hold his sob.

"David . . . oh, Dudie . . . Dudele, Dudele . . ."

A brace of frightened hazel hens burst cover, their chitter following them into a narrow well of morning light.

8

THE SPAN was mismatched. Uphill, the brockled mare—wide-chested, shags of white hair draping its thick shanks to the pasterns—carried the full weight of the wagon, the traces taut, the leather hame cutting into its shoulder. At the mare's side, the sorrel pony frisked—nickering and snuffling—spindleshanks stepping high, its prance never carrying it forward to share the load. Once they'd crested, the britska slanted forward, the wheels rattled freely, and the lagging sorrel bolted, sweeping downhill. The wagon—lurching and tilting to the left—ran up the mare's hocks; the breeching tightened around her haunches, and the checked wagon straightened, left wheels slamming to earth—churning up a twister of dust and grit.

Eyes heavenward, chanting a hymn, Gerhart Paulder rolled with the bucking wagon, the reins loose in his right hand, the left swaying uselessly—like a plumb line—at his side. The rush of cool air under the overhang of trees seemed like balm, and the shrieks of Stepan and Ritter behind like hosannas.

As the wagon jarred level at the foot of the sag, the large cast-iron vat broke loose, scattering the smaller baskets, boxes, jugs, and buckets across the splintered floorboard. Pale as ashes, Stepan followed the scuttling vat with his clear eye, resisting the urge to turn and choke off Ritter's yelps of excitement.

A deep draw elbowed the road into a wide turn, the sorrel dropped back again, and the mare reeled up the slack in the traces. The wagon pitched from side to side, jolted by potholes. Above the creaking and splintering, Paulder interrupted his hymn with a piercing whistle. The mare bore right, rattling over the shoulder of the road onto a level field.

In a mixed stand of oak and elm Paulder reined in. The late-morning sun broke through the maze of limbs and shoots, sideslipping from the straight-boled crowns to the short grass below. Paulder dropped the lines, lifted his face and right arm, and whispered, *"Omnipotens Deus—"*

He glanced over his shoulder at Stepan, who had thrown his hands around the cast-iron soup vat. Hard of hearing, Paulder shouted, as if Stepan were over the next hill, "Save the picnic, not the slop! Do you eat shells and throw away the nuts?"

Gripping the lip of his wooden seat, Paulder lowered his bulk, groping with one leg for the hub, then sliding to the ground. He crossed to the back of the britska and released the hasp holding the gate. He whooped, "Stepan, you bring the blanket and buckle on the feed bag, and you . . . what's your name again?"

"Ritter."

"Ritter, the box with the stamps, and untie the blue jug. The stopper's loose, so don't trip over your feet."

Stepan and Ritter slid off the floorboard. Paulder led the way to the base of a white oak. He pointed to the light leaching through, "Ah-h . . . If light like that ever fell on the great windows of Amiens, Saint Firmin would be sanctified again."

Stepan spread the blanket. Ritter set down the cardboard box with the canceled stamps facing up, but held the dripping jug. Paulder flipped his useless left arm out of the way and said, "Let's see what Hilde-Marie sent this week."

Removing a Swiss army knife from his pocket, he placed it between his knees, pressed against the handle, and pried open the blade with his right hand. "We held Amiens for a while in '14. I was transferred East and then the French came back." Paulder chuckled. "Maybe my leaving gave them courage."

The knife blade slid along the gummed tape sealing the box.

"An unforgettable transept. We don't have anything like it. Nothing. Only a bad imitation at Cologne. Are your hands glued to that, Rittler?"

"Ritter, sir—"

"What's wrong with Rittler, son? Put down the cider. Easy. Good. Now fetch the glasses."

A nosegay of spices debouched from the split at the top of the box. Paulder slid his fingers under the ear of cardboard, loosening the wrapping. He shut his eyes and inhaled, the crow's-feet scoring his temples puckering, his white mustache trembling with need. "Ah-h . . . Hilde-Marie . . ."

He tore open the carton. "In the First War, the packages never got through. This time, we're more organized. We'll win, you'll see." Ritter brought up three glasses, telescoped together. Paulder looked straight at him. "Never underestimate the importance of little things."

"No, sir."

Paulder reached into the carton and drew out a butt of smoked pork, a large Goettinger sausage and a smaller *Mettwurst,* a loaf of dark caraway bread, an apricot *Sachertorte* wrapped in a dishtowel, and a jar of pickled tomatoes, green and red bell peppers, cauliflower, and chickpeas.

"Little things and accidents—"

Paulder pressed his knee into the stump of pork; it slid away. He firmed the butt against a hump in the blanket and sliced off and curled a rasher into his mouth. He smiled teasingly at the two boys, carved another cut, hacked it in half, and pointed with the tip of the blade. Stepan and Ritter ran their "Thank you, sir" together and reached for the cuttings.

"Figure windage wrong and a shell crashes into the Vintage Scene at Reims or the Cloth Hall at Ypres. Doesn't take much. At Amiens, concussion did in the rose window."

Paulder sawed off three slabs of *Mettwurst.* Stepan asked, "Do you build cathedrals?"

Laughing, Paulder said, "No one builds cathedrals. The last one's been built. When this war's over—between this one and the one coming—I'm going to save them."

"How?"

"Not all, understand. The best, in a book." Paulder tore off the heel of the caraway bread and handed the loaf to Stepan. "With Hilde-Marie's help. Besides stuffing her own sausage, she takes pictures."

They ate the pork and the sausage in silence. Stone-flies droned. Bark beetles swarmed over the rough rifts of the white oak. Stepan looked at the sun. How long would Paulder sit under these trees? Had Antanas understood? The Lithuanian had bolted the two small livers—swallowing twice, not chewing, not answering. Stepan had started to repeat: Remember . . . the skinny one with cinnamon hair . . . the vat . . . But Antanas had turned away, lapping the grease off his fingers.

Paulder opened the jar, speared a pickled cauli-flower for Stepan and a red pepper for Ritter; poured cider for the boys and himself and lifted his glass.

"Prosit!"

"Prosit, sir."

Paulder dried the droop of his wet mustache with his wrist and sat back, the first gust of hunger flagging. "It won't be that long. When you two are soldiers, don't listen to fables about bravery and cowardice. Was he shot in the chest or the ass? Twit-tle. Little accidents—"

Stepan said, "Was your arm an accident?"

"Two."

Paulder breathed deeply, expanding his chest to the span of his belly. He let out air, burped, murmured a pleased "Ah-h . . ." and bent to whittle away at the butt and the sausage. Folding the *Mettwurst* into two parings of pork, Paulder fashioned a sandwich with-out bread. He tried to cram it all into his mouth, but was left with a greasy morsel in his fingers. Spraying suet, he said, "Hindenburg had his eye on Warsaw and the Russian Grand Duke on Silesia. At the beginning of October the Russians found our battle order in the wallet of a German officer. A few days later a Russian corpse turned up the Grand Duke's operational plan. How could we lose when we knew their game and how could they lose when they knew ours? Hindenburg struck hard. The Grand Duke launched a massive offensive. Tarnów and Józefów, the San and the Vistula. Back and fill, ride and tie, we ended up where we started, but forty thousand of our men dead."

Ritter said, "You were lucky, sir."

Taking absent stock of Ritter, Paulder bolted the last scraps of pork and sausage.

"Ritter—," the boy reminded him.

Still studying him, Paulder emptied the cider from his glass and shouted, "Who makes the luck?"

Ritter whispered, "I don't know, sir."

"Find out, Ritter! Then you'll know everything. That's all there is! The Who who makes the luck!"

Paulder tried to rise but fell back. Waving off Stepan's help, he puffed, "I'll make my way. Get started."

Stepan filled the carton and folded the four flaps to hold without tape. Ritter telescoped the glasses and rammed the stopper into the jug. Paulder bellowed, "We're letting the horses eat like ostriches!"

Stepan removed the feed bags. Ritter tied the cider jug to a brace. Stepan returned the carton to the wagon and lashed the cast-iron kettle into a corner. Each on one side, they swung up the rear gate, hooked and bolted the hasp over the staple, and waited for Paulder.

Paulder was on his knees, withered arm dangling,

white shaggy head bent into a narrow fall of sunlight, his right hand pressing his forehead. Fervently he whispered, *"Gratias agimus tibi omnipotens Deus pro omnibus beneficiis tuis—"*

9

THE SOUP was cold, salty—and reeked although it lacked fat. Dudie forced himself to gulp the last slimy gruel and with his fingers spaded the ration of marmalade into his mouth. Closing his eyes, he tightened his jaws and locked his tongue against his palate. Slowly the sweetness thinned into his own juices and trickled down to his throat. He coughed, but the choking as well was sweet, and only at the last moment before gagging did he swallow.

Unlike the salty slush, the marmalade gave him strength. The sweat chilling him faded and for the first time Dudie felt the warmth of the sun.

Drawing his knees closer to his chin, he leaned back against the handle of the two-wheeled dumpcart, parked on the trestle over the narrow stream. The sunlight turned white; heat ran into him through his eyelids. He rolled up and put into his mouth half the five-ounce portion of bread—not chewing, saving the bread ball. Reaching under his gray shirt where the two buttons were missing, he tucked the other half under his left armpit.

All morning he'd been sure-footed and steady, picking his way across the drainage ditch, his feet digging into the grade of sand and cinders, the oak cross-sleepers—hewed flat on top and on bottom by the axman, but their natural roughness untouched on the sides—sinking deep into his shoulder as his partner trudged up the embankment, the slope and weight of the ties falling on him. Together they lowered the crossties to the bed of crushed stone and gravel, the buckers urging them to hurry and the placers, holding the lengths of T iron, waiting impatiently to set down their heavy rails. Behind them at the head of the lay-by, carved out of the wood two kilometers from the railroad station, peddlers distributed joint fastenings to the bolters, and maul men spiked rails. Under a spray of shade along the bare embankment where the broken slag was being tamped by a crew swinging shovels, the young sergeant in the baggy uniform dozed beside the engineer—squinting at the blueprint tacked between two linden trees—and the Lithuanian prisoner in gray, his fingers glazed with red paint, for some reason looked elsewhere, never noticing Dudie's energy. Late morning, when the weariness came without warning, draining him, crossing his legs, jiggling his hands, fuzzing his vision, the Lithuanian seemed to follow him with his eyes—the pupils black and dull as coal dust—as if Dudie alone were laying the track.

Before the lunch break, Dudie had looked over his shoulder and ahead, where the ditches and subgrades were being formed. Many prisoners were as young as he, and all had been there longer. None seemed to tire. How did they last? Or did they? Were only the strong working? What happened to the weak? Was there a hospital—or another camp—where he could work sitting?

He didn't think so. The sergeant with the cap falling over his eyes, the Lithuanian and the engineer, the two corporals behind their machine guns, saw only track—and either bustling or lagging. Never did they talk to prisoners; they barked or prodded. Whom would he ask, "Sir, is there a hospital?"

He had seen the other prisoners split their bread ration, hiding a small lump for the afternoon, and if he weakened later, the bread under his armpit would help. When he bent over to lift a cross-sleeper, he could slip his fingers past the missing buttons . . .

He groped with his tongue for the bread ball. The cold sweat—and with it the shakiness—returned. With his mind wandering, he couldn't remember chewing or putting down half of his day's bread. He swept his memory, but couldn't recall the taste at all.

Opening his eyes, he drew in the heat of the sun, and when the pain of the light throbbed in his temple Dudie looked to the side, into the open sky, as the two of them used to, laughing and comparing specks dancing—which each knew he had turned loose—until Momma called.

When the specks faded, he stared again at the sun—feeling stronger—and hoped, if it were still early in the lunch hour, to store up enough heat to ward off during the afternoon the sweat that chilled and frightened.

In addition to storing heat, he must purge thoughts of fear, thought of bread, thought of fainting, and give a stiff finger to the Lithuanian, to the sergeant, to the engineer, to the britska driver with the shriveled arm and the voice like geese in the ear. He must move away from himself, away from panic, and imagine instead how his friends would have mimicked the Lithuanian's silly stutter and what they would have guessed the sergeant carried in the seat of his baggy pants.

"F-f-for what?"

How much could he allow himself to be bullied by a Lithuanian who can't wrap his tongue around an "f"?

"Rations!" The britska driver honked the word.

"H-how m-m-many?" the Lithuanian asked.

"Two hundred eight."

"H-how do I kn-know, I didn't c-c-count."

"Take my word."

"D-did you? D-did you c-count?"

"I don't have to. I believe what I read. If you could read, you'd believe—so believe you can read and believe you believe what it says."

"S-say that s-slower—"

"Take the pen!"

A cloud coasted by. The brief slide of shade chilled Dudie. Dropping his head forward from its prop on the handle of the two-wheeled cart, he listened to the water slipping underneath the trestle and felt the sun's warmth roll across the nape of his neck.

"Th-there."

"There? Can you prove your name is X?"

"D-don't b-be f-f-funny."

"Friend Antanas, remember you're one of them, not us. Give me back my pen and a grunt to clean the pot."

"W-why c-clean the pot? They're l-l-less restless w-with a k-k-k-kiss of d-dysentery."

"Work out your own dysentery. A dirty pot draws flies and flies bite my horse."

Dudie heard the cast-iron vat scrape along the

ground. The Lithuanian laughed. A bird called from
a tree and an Alsatian barked in answer. A large fly
droned near his ear, waned, drifted closer. The fly's
thrum turned into his mother's nasal lullaby:

שלאָף מײַן קינד, מײַן טרײסט, מײַן שײנער
שלאָף זשע זונעניו ...

The kick swept away his feet. Dudie fell to the side,
hitting the ground hard with his elbow. Squinting up,
he felt through the tear in the sleeve and soothed the
bruise.

"Your turn. Ten minutes."

"Ten minutes—going, coming, cleaning."

The two blond boys who had come with the britska
stood over him, holding the vat between them.

Dudie looked up from the leather sandals and the
hobnailed boots and rose to his feet. He knew straightening his elbow would hurt, but the pain was sharper
than he expected.

They dropped the vat. The new boy in the boots
said, "Are you waiting for someone?"

Dudie tried to lift the vat, but his arms were too
short. Gripping one handle with both hands, he tried
to drag the kettle. The boy he'd seen before with the
cheekbone missing circled with his finger, "On its
side."

The new boy followed, the other remaining behind,
standing near the dumpcart.

The rolling vat sheered away each time it bumped
over one of its handles. The bottom of the kettle was
slippery and heavy, and difficult to straighten. Once,
he glanced over his shoulder, appealing for help, but

the eyes of the boy under the straight fall of flax hair remained cold.

He tumbled the vat past a knot of maul men, a few napping, others facing but not seeing him, their eyes glazed. Above the sandpit the heavy kettle slipped out of his grip, banging and clattering down the grade. He hurried after it, expecting but not hearing abuse from the boy behind.

The vat came to rest on its bottom in the deep drainage ditch. Straining, Dudie tried to hoist, then to push it toward the sandpit over the shoulder. Suddenly the vat arched and pitched into the sand.

The boy stood at the edge of the pit, the sun behind him. In his right hand, which had swung the heavy vat, he balled a patch of rough burlap. Tossing it, the boy said, "Let me see your ass and your elbows."

Dudie caught the burlap and slid down the drainage ditch and into the sandpit. He scooped several fistsful of grit into the vat and crawled inside, scrubbing with the coarse brown cloth; he held his breath against the maggoty fumes.

"Don't turn around. Listen. No matter what you hear, keep scraping away."

Sounds rumbled strangely in the vat. Had he heard right? Had he heard anything? Was the boy standing at the edge of the pit speaking to *him*?

"Don't turn!"

Reaching behind, Dudie bucked fresh sand into the vat. Again, the boy's voice throbbed in the kettle.

"Your name's Fehrmann."

"How do you know?"

"Your brother sent me."

"He's dead—"

"Dummy up, or I'll kill you! Asshead, ears open and mouth closed. Your brother was told to play dead. Your mother pushed him off the train into a stack of corpses. She died here of typhus. Your father was dead already. He—your father was in the stack."

"How does Perchik know I'm here?"

"Paulder's calling. Finish quickly."

"Where is he?"

Dudie waited for an answer, grinding the burlap and sand against the last of the sludge.

"Where's Perchik? Please—"

Backing out, Dudie looked around. The boy was gone. Along the embankment, spikers and bolters trudged to their places. Who was he? Would Dudie ever see him again? Had Dudie imagined the conversation? No, Dudie knew he'd spoken, was sure he'd heard the boy. Whispering, he tried to repeat what he'd said, what was said to him, but he couldn't remember the order, or the words exactly. Momma and Poppa were dead. Perchik . . . Was Perchik alive, *still* alive? *Was* he? Had the boy said he was? Had the boy said "Perchik," or had Dudie put together his brother's name out of sounds booming in the vat?

A whistle blew; the lunch hour was over. Dudie wondered how he'd drag the vat out of the pit and back to the wagon. Somehow he managed to grip the kettle by both handles, but he let loose and pinched a few grains of greasy sand between his fingers.

In his pocket he hid the precious grit from the ground where the boy who knew his brother had stood, and then he turned again to grapple with the vat.

I O

WHEN you waited, light was as slow going as coming. First glow seemed always too shy to break in, and the last now too snug to leave. Perchik called hoarsely, lifting his voice in a wail, ending with a fox's bark, and after a moment answering himself with the three short yips of a vixen. If he shook loose night life, time might pass quicker. He waited, but roused only the large Rottweiler who stood—bracing his forepaws against the chain-link fence—and bayed at the early moon.

"You're as big an asshead as your brother."

Ritter's kick hurt. Perchik rubbed his calf soothingly in the damp grass. The heavy-boned dog dropped from sight and Perchik slithered forward, ahead of Ritter, to the edge of the clearing of mimosa.

"Far enough," Ritter warned.

Perchik pressed down a cluster of tufted vetch. The half-timbered house stood alone in the clearing, squared by the fence, overhung by a towering poplar tree, the roof of new cedar shingles sloping steeply to shed drifts of snow. The house seemed abandoned. White paint flaked. Scrub—clumps of wild privet and chickweed—smothered the garden, and the path to the front gate faded into a thick broom of wire and switch grass.

"Maybe they took him away, too," Perchik said.

"No, the mayor looks fed."

"Who's the mayor?"

"My dog."

Again, the huge Rottweiler lifted to his hind feet, his forepaws locked into the fence, his nose high, sniffing.

"Does he work in the camp?" Perchik whispered.

"No, in town. He's an official of some kind. He receives and sends briefcases full of papers. If they're correct, he puts on stamps and seals and scratches his name with my uncle's goose-quill pen."

"Sounds important."

"Erich Heyler—"

"Don't look at me, Ritterhof. I don't know anybody."

"He brought a uniform, but he's not a soldier. I saw him put it on once for a parade."

"That's a big house for one man."

"He's not always alone. Sometimes he has women. I used to peek in on him—at my uncle's desk—but the bedrooms are upstairs. He swings his ass when he walks, and his women have short haircuts and mustaches."

"That sounds funny."

"I used to come back to the house a lot, in the beginning."

"That sure sounds funny. Mustaches?"

"To me, too. How can we get up to my window for a peek?"

Perchik measured across the crown of the poplar tree to the dormer. The tree was tall enough, but during the day the window would reflect, and in the evening curtains shield.

"More than one girl at a time?" Perchik asked.

"Always more."

"I don't like Erich Heyler."

"I hate him. He's the one who arrested my uncle."

"I don't like the sound of his name."

"He didn't say one word to me. He showed respect for my uncle. Swore he didn't have to pack, he'd be back. As soon as my uncle was gone, Heyler grabbed me by the ear and dragged me out."

"Men like that and girls with mustaches turn my stomach."

"Never said a word. Just slam slammed the door."

The Rottweiler dropped his front paws to the ground. Black and tan, he was indistinct in the graying light against the wood gallery circling the house. Perchik said, "Are you sure Heyler's not there?"

"If he is, he'll turn the lights on."

"If he isn't, he might come home after you go in."

"That's the chance."

"Take me—"

"No. Heyler knows I'm out here. To them you're dead. You better stay dead."

Perchik laughed and kicked out playfully at Ritter. "Nobody's better dead." Then he added, "Asshead."

Ritter sat and unwound the laces of his hobnailed boots.

Perchik asked, "What if you get caught?"

"I'll be punished for stealing from myself."

"How much will you take?"

"Two bottles, if that bastard hasn't finished the champagne."

"Champagne?"

"My uncle was wounded in France. One of the first —but he got there first."

Ritter stood, in his stocking feet, two elf toes poking through ragged holes. Beside him, Perchik rose to his knees. In the lowering shadow of the mimosa, the spray of vetch now was indistinct. The sky sheathed the poplar and the cedar roof—only the blur of flaking white paint showing. Reaching down, Ritter touched Perchik lightly on the shoulder and moved off into the darkness along the tree line.

To Perchik, Ritter's home seemed a mansion, an air castle floating on fresh breezes and tall grass. Their apartment—Momma and Poppa's bedroom, the Doulton stove filling the kitchen alcove, the sitting room where he and Dudie slept on the ottoman—had been no larger than Ritter's attic.

His father had been a merchant. Perchik wasn't sure what Jakob did. He bought and sold, and other people spent the money he was whispered to have hidden in a prayer book. Weren't Socialists such as Ritter's uncle laborers, and weren't they supposed to live in sixth-floor walk-ups overlooking courtyards hung with laundry that never dried, tossing rubbish from windows, getting rid of the garbage but never the smell? And wasn't a merchant such as his father cut out to be a country gentleman, living in a half-timbered house, each of his sons in his own bedroom, one overlooking a towering poplar tree, the other a grove of mimosa? Nothing he'd ever heard or read seemed true. Everything was damp side up, dry side down. He was sure only of Ritter's friendship, of their pit, of the forest . . . and now of Dudie.

For a while, he had forgotten that anything had come before. It seemed he and Ritter had been in their wood always, he hiding, Ritter bringing sugar and salt and traps from the outside. They would continue this way day by day, nothing changing, not growing older, until the world froze over or dried up. Now he remembered—a dark vestibule, wooden stairs worn slippery, a father Jakob and a mother Miriam, a young brother—and remembering depressed him, because he knew that for Dudie's sake he must look ahead, and he had forgotten how.

Perchik heard the dog's warning bark turn to a whine; Ritter was over the fence, hugging his mayor. The windows remained dark. Erich Heyler had not come home, and in a few minutes he would be too late.

Erich.

Erich Heyler.

Did an Erich live with his family in their flat? Was the father another merchant? Did his two children sleep on an ottoman in the sitting room? Did the mother steal in, winter mornings, and reach under the worn duck-down cover, slipping rough wool socks over skinny legs, so the boys would not leave the warmth of the quilt bare? Did the father terrorize the mother—complaining of the cold, the lack of food, shouting at her for the stupidity of statesmen—and stand in awe of his two small sons, touching them rarely, and only on the head, trying to put all his love into a ruffle of hair?

A door stopped in mid-creak. Perchik pictured Ritter, alarmed, holding the door in place, squeezing by. The mayor whimpered. Did he want to cram through, too? Was Ritter hissing "tsh-sh"?

Then, not a sound; until a mole cricket burst into a long burr and took off in front of Perchik, its hind wings twitching clumsily.

Although the boy standing on the platform had looked different—thinner, paler, hair darker—Perchik had been sure it was his brother. But how could he be Dudel? They'd left Dudie behind—safe. At least one of them would survive. His father had explained to Perchik, tears running into his mouth, spitting them out in anger, anger at himself, his task, their neighbor Theo. As if it were a favor, Theo had taken everything from them—furniture, cash, wedding rings, gilt picture frames, torn quilts—and promised to hide one, not two (two would talk, or laugh, or pick at each other), until the war was over. And Jakob, weeping, slurring, fighting the words, hating their meaning, stumbled from one half sentence to another: he felt like the foolish man in Job, his habitation cursed, his children crushed in the gate . . . Dudie was the younger . . . the sicklier . . . who knew what lay ahead in the transfer camp . . . Ending with a great bellow, a screaming "NO!" and pressing Perchik's head to his chest.

What had gone wrong? Everything had been arranged. Paid for. Agreed to. Accepted. Had Theo betrayed them as soon as Dudie turned from a bribe into a risk? Would the Lithuanian guard do the same, once he'd sucked dry the bottles of French champagne? What choice did Momma and Poppa have; did he have now? The Lithuanian, like Theo, was an only hope. Even as an infant, Dudie had been frail, pale, weak. How long could he drag railroad ties?

Ahead, a shadow crossed against the movement of leaves bending with the wind. Perchik rose to his feet and slid off into the thicket of mimosa.

Ritter, padding silently, started when Perchik stepped to his side. "Where'd you come from?"

"Did you find champagne?" Perchik asked.

"Don't do—ever do—that again."

"Ritter—"

"My uncle said, the best. Heyler will miss it for sure."

Ritter started to run. Reaching out, Perchik held him by the arm and tugged at the two bottles. "I trust you with my life, Ritter von Ritterhof, but you better let me carry the schnapps."

I I

PERCHIK closed his eyes. Across the shoal a smoke-dry branch snapped. Perchik bent the stave and slid the sinew along the yew until the string bit into the notch. His prey broke from the thick growth of goat willow. Perchik drew an arrow from the birch-bark quiver, braced his left knee on the ground, and cocked his right. Theo Seldz bolted into a hedge of osier. The green and white leaves trembled and then Dudie cried out, crawled from his sinkhole among the roots, and ran. Theo clutched. Dudie squirmed, kicked free, and splashed into the wallow, wading toward Perchik. Canting his bow, Perchik loosed. The point arched and as Theo reached the water's edge he seemed to lurch into the arrow's pile. The shaft sank deep into his rib cage and after a single chuck of air Theo Seldz pitched face forward. Dudie looked toward Perchik gratefully, but then turned and raced into his mother's arms. Jakob rose from the ottoman and stood, stealing glances at Perchik—half smiling— but too shy to cross the sitting room to put his pride for his son into words.

Perchik shook Theo Seldz out of his head and half opened his eyelids. Under a parching sun in the pocket below, Dudie strained, but couldn't lift the sheet-iron pail. The Lithuanian guard had been as good as his word, his word matching his fire for the looted French champagne. He would take the risk and rid Dudie of the crushing weight of the oak crossties. Now would Perchik and Ritter have to go back to steal schnapps for Dudie's new partner?

His hair long to his shoulders, bare-chested, arms and legs thick as a boar, he strode up and down the bed of stone and gravel, head thrown back, hooting, "Now or never! Listen to Semyon! It's now! Do you hear? Now or never!"

Dudie scrambled after Semyon, the sheet-iron pail dropping lower and lower as the morning wormed along, trying to lift the bucket to Semyon's groping fingers whenever the giant bawled, "Spikes!"

Semyon never looked down at Dudie; Dudie had to be there. The giant flung the spikes at the bolters, who scrambled to pluck the sailing skewers from the air; and the higher Semyon's eyes soared into the sky, the lower Dudie's shoulders sagged toward the ground.

Perchik plucked and chewed on a blade of spear grass. A swarm of brown mussel scales were gorging on a fallen chip of alder, leaving a scar oozing sap and smelling of damp shavings. Perchik slid the end of his yew bow under the sprig and flipped. Spraying scales, the bough fell into a tumble of hairless dwarf thistle.

"Bolts! Here! Right here, now or never!"

Dudie faded to his knees.

"Bolts, pup!"

Why didn't Semyon help? He could lift the pail—or Dudie—with his little finger.

In desperation, Dudie wrenched himself erect. The handle tore into his fingers, his shoulders shuddered—but the bucket cleared the ground. Semyon looked down. The bucket did not reach his hand; he would have to bend.

"Now or never, pup . . . wake up!"

At Semyon's bellow, the sergeant opened his eyes and rose to his feet, his trousers unsticking slowly from his sweating rump and unfurling as if caught in a gust.

Semyon leaned over, closed his huge fingers over a grab of spikes, and scattered them toward the bolters. "Up!"

The Lithuanian lifted his head and Perchik saw him look nervously to the young sergeant blinking sleepily under the linden tree. Ritter and Stepan, one on each side of the cart driver with the crippled arm, shoved the soup vat to the center of the serving table. Stepping to the side, Ritter faced the sergeant as he shuffled into the sun. With a wag of his elbow, Ritter tipped over the stack of soup tins. The clatter set off a flurry of squawks and fluttering in the forest. Spinning, the sergeant snapped an order to the driver, who whipped his good arm across Ritter's ear. Ritter tumbled to the ground, gashing his wrist on the loose shale, rolling over and squeezing his arm to dull the pain. The sergeant clumped toward Ritter, shaking his fist and cursing. Perchik wished he could rush forward to help Ritter, and to tell him; he had become Perchik and Dudie's third brother.

Semyon swung along the rails, gleaming in a slow curve, Dudie close behind, bent in half, the heavy bucket clearing the ground by a spider's thread.

Semyon reached the rail end and with a "Het!" tossed the final skewer to the last bolter as the lunch whistle shrilled. Shovels clanged to the ground and carts dropped in place. The prisoners pushed their wilted limbs to a scuffle and lined up behind the serving table.

Spikes and rails, crossties, joint fastenings, lining bars, rooters, and prypoles littered the lay-by carved out of the wood. The embankment, the drainage ditches, the grades, and the subgrades were suddenly silent and desolate. A flick of rust-colored hair caught Perchik's eye, and then he saw that Dudie had not been carried along in the shuffle. On his knees, shoulders drooping, head bowed, Dudie huddled in front of his sheet-iron pail, shivering in the midday sun.

Perchik wanted to jump up and run to the edge of the tree line—to signal quickly to Dudie, to whisper, to shout. Hadn't Dudie heard the whistle? Did he expect to work through the afternoon without eating? How could he be cold when everyone was running sweat? Dudie was tired—and weak—but why was he numb? How much strength would it take to lift his head, to place his hand on the rim of the bucket for support, to push himself up? Pushing is easy. Dudie, *push!* Let the bucket do the work. Dear sweet stupid little brother . . . *move!*

A spasm ripped through Dudie's body. His chin fell forward to his chest. He seemed asleep on his knees. Prisoners returning from the serving table passed on either side of him, and sat along the rails, on stacked crossties, on hummocks of gravel. A few sipped the gruel as they walked, others peered into their tins, putting off the start and delaying the end of the meal.

None turned to Dudie, but their heads jerked toward the sergeant at his shout.

Clenching his fist, his head thrust forward, the sergeant stormed out of the shade of the linden tree and bounced up the embankment. Without slowing, he scooped up and shook a slab of wood at Dudie.

"You there! Who is that?"

The Lithuanian guard, sitting beside a corporal oiling the bore of his machine gun, dropped his soup tin and scuttled across the path of the sergeant. "I'll s-see t-to him, s-s-sir."

The Lithuanian swung behind Dudie, his right hand —mottled red with paint—rose and came down with a resounding thwack against his own thigh.

"D-d-didn't you h-hear the s-s-sergeant? W-w-what's the w-whistle f-for?"

Dudie started to shiver.

"I'm w-w-w-waiting—"

Again the mottled hand rose. This time it did not come down against the Lithuanian, but cracked across Dudie's ear. Toppling over, Dudie rolled to his back. He did not cry out. His face showed no pain. His eyes locked on the empty sky beyond the guard, and his jaw slacked open, as if it were less painful to draw in this muddle through his mouth.

Perchik rose to his knees, notched the sinew into his stave, and slid an arrow from the quiver. Perchik drew as the Lithuanian wrapped his hand around Dudie's thin arm and lifted as if he were holding a hare by the forepaw. Dudie did not look at the guard but kept his eyes on the sky. When the Lithuanian dropped him to the ground in front of the serving table, Dudie landed on his feet. For a moment he sagged, but then his knees straightened and he stood. The Lithuanian, grinning, joined the sergeant, and together they strolled to the shade of the linden tree. Perchik tracked both—first one, then the other—certain he could bury the pile of his arrow into the back of either man's neck. Glancing at Dudie, he saw his brother holding up his tin. With his good arm the driver ladled out a dipper of gruel. Perchik eased the bowstring.

Dudie sat in the sun near the britska and ate. He chewed slowly, his head pitched back, following a thin cloud in the distance.

Perchik traced along Dudie's eyeline. He felt cold at the thought of the wind driving the tatter of white. The cloud looked like a bat in flight, tipping into its somersault. But Dudie—Perchik remembered . . . they'd been on the roof, the tar paper warm under their backs. Dudie had guessed the cloud was a crane or a swan, coming to save him from talk of Theo Seldz's dark closet, and to take him to America, where he would become rich overnight and send for Momma and Poppa, and Perchik, too—if Perchik never again would laugh at him.

"Why shouldn't I laugh?" Perchik teased.

"Because we're brothers."

"You can be my brother and still be silly."

"I can also be right."

"You're not."

"How do you know so much?"

"I'm older."

Dudie thought a moment, and said stubbornly, "You can be older and be wrong."

"Can be can't be. Cranes don't carry people, even to America."

"I saw a picture."

"A drawing, not a picture. And not everyone's rich in America."

"I'll be—"

"You're looking for a pinch, Dudie."

"I'll tell Momma—"

"Go tell."

"You go. I was here first. And I saw the cloud first. Go find your own."

"Pot-walloper—"

His lids started to part, but then he saw the hob-nailed boots and the leather sandals and clamped shut.

"Your turn again."

The kick to his ribs drove Dudie's breath out. They held the soup vat lightly between them, and the boy who had told him Perchik was alive said, "We're on your time, asshead."

He gripped Dudie by the wrist and pulled him up, clamping Dudie's fingers over the vat handle to re-place his own. The boy in the leather sandals and hop-sack trousers continued to hold up his end, and moved away, carrying the vat alone and dragging Dudie along. They passed the sandpit, picked up the narrow stream bubbling under the trestle, and followed the run of water into the wood. As they crossed into the shade, the boy with the flax hair fell behind and shouted loudly, facing the camp, "Ten minutes, and we expect it to shine!"

In the forest, dead fingers of branches—sharp and

brittle—caught on Dudie's arms and face and snapped off. Dudie lowered his head and followed the boy tugging on the vat until he felt him stop. Looking up, Dudie saw a hill ahead, and in the thick stand of trees a lip of rock damming the stream, which lapped over in a lazy waterfall. Leaving him, the two boys waded into the brook, one holding the vat, the other a pad of steel wool.

They dunked their heads and came up laughing. Soaked, the steel wool soared through the air, hit the rim, and dropped into the vat.

"Score!"

Ringing in fright at the hubbub, a flock of migrating curlew broke cover, circled overhead, and swept into the sun.

The two boys disappeared, swimming downstream. Tilting, the vat drifted with the current after them.

Riding its narrow banks, the stream sloshed gently. The forest was quiet.

"Dudele—"

Dudie turned.

Hair long, lederhosen and thin shirt torn, rags wrapped around his legs and feet, his brother waited in front of a whitebeam. Perchik's eyes were wild, like an animal's; a hunter's bow and quiver slung over his shoulder.

"Dudel . . . come—"

Dudie ran and fell into Perchik's arms, his head resting under his brother's chin. With one hand Perchik pressed Dudie to him, with the other he rumpled his hair.

I 2

THE PILE struck with a dull thunk. Blood blowing from the spit large artery, the young buck broke stride and sagged, but recovered and bolted forward.

Head down, his Solingen knife drawn, Ritter pushed into the skirt of hop. "The ribs are mine if I hamstring him before you throw in a second arrow."

Perchik reached out and pulled Ritter down beside him.

In the distance, the crack and brush of leaves faded.

Perchik whispered, "Let him make his run."

For a moment the forest was dead—soundless—and then a warbler called, a hidden and short "tirk."

Perchik let out his breath. The full sun would be strong. The deer would be his. By tomorrow, this buck would be dressed and cooled enough to eat.

Gingerly, Ritter touched the cheesecloth wrapped around his left wrist where the flecks of red showed.

"For hitting me, we'll give that bastard Paulder the gullet stuffed with blowflies."

"I'd almost given up." Perchik stood and removed an arrow from the birchbark quiver. "Ritter—for Paulder blowflies, but for everyone else this venison won't need a thing. A few juniper berries, maybe."

Perchik turned slowly, listening. Ritter asked, "Has he stopped somewhere?"

Perchik shook his head.

"Will he get away?"

"No."

Perchik leaned heavily, first to the right, then to the left, squeezing out the dew soaked up during the night into the burlap covering his tennis shoes. "Keep your eyes to your side. I'll watch mine."

Holding the yew bow clamped under his arm, Perchik retied the rope cinching the gray prison trousers drawn over his lederhosen, and stepped into the small clearing.

The hoofprints of the deer—each set the shape of matched teardrops—were visible in the soft ground. Blood—caking and black—studded the trampled sallow. Moving rapidly but silently, Perchik followed the trail. Ritter hurried along at his heels, his eyes fixed to the right.

Perchik led the way through a thick cluster of sow thistle, cut a narrow field of milkwort, crossed the stream, and on recrossing startled a nest of young crake. When the flutter stilled, Perchik stopped. He motioned to Ritter to stand steady.

Ritter heard no sound and saw no movement, but Perchik leaned slightly into the chill morning wind, his knuckles clenched over the bow and around the nock, listening and sniffling—sensing his prey.

A cone dropped from a larch. Lacewings fluttered. Lazily, the stream flushed its banks.

Perchik took one cautious step and the deer, circled back on its trail, rose stiffly to its knees. Perchik spun and loosed. The string shrilled. The point of the arrow punched into the deer behind the shoulder, driving through the heart and into the lungs.

The buck dropped, its head rolling to the side and cracking into a spike of burstone.

Still holding his Solingen knife, Ritter crammed an earsplitting whistle through his teeth and broke into a jig. He danced around Perchik, then stooped under Perchik's elbows, locked his arms around his waist, and lifted. Whirling Perchik in a circle, Ritter whooped: "Hey, hey, hey! Mighty, mighty, mighty midget hunter!"

Perchik leaned down and said, "Asshead," but the spinning ground made him dizzy, and he tipped back and felt his face cutting cool air, and closed his eyes against the reeling sky. He smiled and saw the blue ceiling of a kitchen alcove, the paint bubbled with dampness and streaked with soot, and Jakob in front of the old Doulton, trying to be heard above Ritter's babble, reaching out timidly to Ritter, his lips moving, pleading, "Let me . . . let me play with him—"

Suddenly, Ritter opened his arms. Perchik dropped to the ground, buckling his legs to blunt the fall. Perchik lowered his forehead to his kneecaps and started to laugh. Ritter slumped down beside him. Winded, he rested his head on Perchik's back and chuckled. "Mighty, mighty, mighty brother—"

Perchik sniffed and lifted his head. Excreta running from the deer spread in a widening pock. A nauseating waft of urine stopped his nostrils.

"Ritter," Perchik said, "the buck hasn't given up. If we don't move, he can win yet."

Perchik withdrew the arrows; one had snapped off

at the footing. They tugged and jostled the deer, and on a slight grade turned the buck on its back, head uphill. Under the hips and shoulders they wedged rocks to keep the buck from rolling over. With his Solingen, Ritter sliced off the scrotum. Holding the testicles between thumb and forefinger, he shouted, "For Commandant Hoegel!"

Perchik took the knife from Ritter and peeled off the skin on the inside hock of the buck's hind leg. The musk gland yielded a greenish fluid, overwhelming the stenches of urine and feces.

Coughing, Perchik said, "For Stepan, to rub into Hoegel's eyes!"

Tossing aside the testicles, Ritter reached for the knife, sank it two inches into the flesh beside the anal vent, and ripped in a circle. "And one night I'm coming for you . . . Erich Heyler—"

Smeared with blood, Ritter held out the handle of the knife to Perchik.

Perchik asked, "What's his name again?"

"Who?"

Perchik rammed the blade into the abdomen above the pelvic bone, grunting with the frenzy of the thrust.

"The Lithuanian."

"Antanas."

Sawing rapidly, Perchik gritted his teeth. "If anything happens to Dudie—"

Inserting two fingers in the opening to brace the abdominal flap, careful not to puncture the intestines or stomach, Perchik split the buck to its rib cage. "Antanas," he whispered fiercely, "if Dudie's scratched, you bleed."

When Perchik straightened—his face set—Ritter,

too, had stopped frisking. He said, "Let's wash our hands and get to work."

Quickly, Perchik removed the second musk gland and the two glands on the buck's other hind leg. He tied off the penis and the anal vent, and then he and Ritter ran to the stream and cleaned the Solingen and the unbroken arrow and scrubbed their hands with mud and shingle.

When they returned to the deer, flies were buzzing over the carcass. Working swiftly, Perchik slashed the pelvis between the two hams, opened the rib cage, and slit the neck to the jawbone. He removed the gullet and cut the viscera loose along the spine and dia-phragm. After hacking out and putting aside the heart and the liver, he tucked the knife under the rope belting his trousers and smeared the blood collected in the chest cavity over the exposed flesh to glaze. He and Ritter dragged the carcass through the forest to a spruce and hung the young buck by its head. With boughs, they spread the abdominal cavity to air and dry, and scattered branches thickly over the carcass where the glaze would not be thick enough to seal the flesh against jays and magpies.

Breathing heavily, spent, Perchik led the way to the stream and they washed again. Ritter stretched out on the bank, away from the stench of the carcass and the entrails, and Perchik returned to guard the buck hang-ing in the spruce. He leaned against the trunk, closed his eyes, and slumped slowly to the ground.

Perchik's eyelids drooped, his head fell to the side, and he wondered why he felt warm under the cool overhang of shading branches. Forcing his lids open did not stop his tumble to the comfort of sleep. He stood and rubbed his fingers through his tangled hair, scratching briskly. He would have to be up again all night. Better to sleep late in the afternoon.

Perchik walked to the stream. Ritter had rolled to the side, pinning his hand. When he awoke, the arm would hang, asleep. Carefully, Perchik knelt, but Ritter felt the movement. He smiled and mumbled, "Hey, mighty hunter—"

Perchik rolled Ritter to his stomach. Ritter grunted, stretched his freed arm, and clenched and unclenched his fingers. He said, "Another minute—" and dozed off.

Perchik found a split of flat shale at the water's edge and carefully whetted Ritter's Solingen. His father, he remembered, hid a flat stone and a small can of machine oil in the armoire behind the camphored sheets that preserved Miriam's wedding dress. Jakob brought home a broken knife he'd found in the street —who would buy such a thing?—and each Friday before sunset in a corner of the flat he would hone the single blade and pare his nails. Momma objected. Making dirt in public was vulgar. Jakob agreed; he would be happy to clean his nails in private. Where?

Perchik tested the cutting edge of the Solingen against his nail and then dipped the nib into the stream and filed the tip in a smooth circle against the shale.

Before Dudie came, he'd rarely thought of Jakob apart from Dudie and Miriam. His mother also was dead, and Dudie's life hung by its head in a tree, but Jakob now would not leave him. He seemed more real in Perchik's half-dreams than he had been in the sixth-floor walk-up. At times Perchik wished his father away, but Jakob strayed in and out like swamp fog. Wouldn't it be easier not to remember your father, like Ritter—or to have had a father who had been close . . . and warm . . . and *there?* Jakob always had been just out of reach—waiting—never stepping forward. Why hadn't he? But why hadn't Perchik? Why had he never said aloud the words beating in his head: "Take my hand, Poppa. Touch me. No one's looking, Poppa. Kiss me—"

Perchik tossed away the shale. Still holding the knife, he strayed through the forest. At a young ash he whittled off a straight branch with few twigs. Returning to the hung buck, he studied the carcass, sniffed approvingly, and sat nearby on a burned-out stump.

Perchik shortened the branch, cutting off the clusters of young shoots at both ends that would leave pins and weaken the arrow. He held the shaft in its length against his eye, then placed the point on the ground and pressed down. The ash was straight and bent evenly. Perchik started to shave away the bark.

Perchik hoped that his and Ritter's presence, and the man-scent left by their tramping, would warn off badgers and otters, and that by this time tomorrow the deer would be delivered, the animal heat cooled out even from the heavy hip and shoulder bones.

He hoped, too, that Ritter was right. Tonight, Ritter had said, he would see Stepan, and again send Stepan to Antanas. The Lithuanian had taken the hare livers and the schnapps. He would snap at the venison;

would have to gorge himself to beat spoilage. He would be promised more—later. Ritter said Antanas couldn't read and didn't know any of the work gang by name. Perchik easily could become Dudie, as long as Antanas was assured that the heads clustered in tens equaled the number of rations—and if anyone in the work gang smirked that overnight Dudie had grown taller and broader, the taste of venison-to-come on Antanas's tongue would prod him to muzzle the prisoner.

Scraping carefully, Perchik smoothed one tip of the new green arrow, shaping a light bulge at the bottom for the nock. He turned his left palm upward and joined his thumb and middle finger. Resting the arrow on his nails, he twisted the ash shaft sharply. Well balanced, it spun smoothly. Before Ritter woke, he would prepare the arrow for feathering, and when Ritter took his turn later under the spruce, Perchik would return to their pit, bury the shaft in the trench stove, and let it dry slowly beside a low fire.

Now that he had flushed the buck, Perchik had hope for his plan, hope that tomorrow night Dudie would sleep in the pit and Perchik in the camp. Perchik feared that closing in Dudie under the crawl-hole might bring on nightmares; and that the creatures prowling overhead—with their snorts, grunts, whines, and yips—might frighten him. Ritter said if Dudie were freed he'd sleep lightly, and be Dudie's brother for Perchik while Perchik was gone.

Dudie would need weeks to regain his strength. Perchik thought again of the possibility that Dudie would buckle during the day—this one day they needed to cure the venison for Antanas—and shook his head; Dudie would live through today because living through meant living on. Dudie would last to the end; anyone could last to the end when the end could be counted in hours edging closer.

Yesterday, waiting behind the whitebeam, Perchik had been surprised. Dudie had not grown; beside Ritter and Stepan he seemed shorter than Perchik remembered. Ritter and Stepan had waded into the brook, playing and laughing, frightening a flock of curlew, but Perchik had hung back, studying his brother. The curlew circled away and the boys splashed downstream and Dudie stood alone in the silence, shivering. When Perchik stepped out, he had thought Dudie was trembling with excitement, but when he came close he saw fright. Perchik had supported him under the armpit with his free hand and lowered him to the ground in the sunlight under a red beech.

Dudie's skin was the color of fresh sap, spit ran from his mouth, and he couldn't lift his twitching hand to wipe away the dribble. With the sleeve of his thin cotton shirt, Perchik reached out and mopped Dudie clean.

"Dudel . . . I won't leave you again—"

"Perchik?"

"Yes—"

"Is it you, Perchik?"

"It's me."

"I wanted to die, Perchik."

"You won't die, Dudel—"

"Not now, now that I've found you. In Theo's closet. I prayed, Perchik. For air, for sun—"

Dudie started to weep. He bent his head in shame. Tears broke from his cheeks to his chin. Perchik this time did not touch him and Dudie choked and fought for his voice.

"—for anything from outside. I used to spend hours —maybe days—with my nose on the floor, trying to breathe air, choking on dust."

"We'll go home, Dudel. We'll find Theo Seldz and I'll kill him."

Dudie shook his head.

"I know how, Dudie."

"Home—"

Dudie crinkled his forehead, trying to remember something, then said, "Never."

Leaning across his feet, which were tucked under him, Dudie touched his brother.

"Perchik—"

"What is it, Dudel?"

" 'Dudel'—I never thought I'd hear my name again." He rubbed Perchik along the arm. "After Theo's closet—I can't live in the sun, either. When I'm tired, I close my eyes and in a second I'm asleep. Or think I'm asleep. I'm not sure. Hours seem to go by. I've dreamed. I've rested. Maybe now we're close to lunch. Or the whistle at the end of the day. I feel so much better, I'm ready to run to the barrack. But I've taken only two steps, Perchik. Or three. And the wood on my back is heavier . . . even the bucket—"

"I saw."

"Perchik?"

"Yes, Dudie."

"I'm weak, Perchik."

Perchik felt as if Dudie's tears had moved to his own throat.

Dudie said, "Soon I'll be dead."

"We'll help."

"I can't live in the dark . . . or in the light. There's nothing else, Perchik. I can't—"

"I'll find a way."

"How?"

"With my friend. We'll think of something."

Perchik had told Dudie to lie down, and Perchik swept away the droning midges until Ritter and Stepan came back with the scrubbed vat. Returning to the whitebeam, Perchik had watched them cross the stream under the trestle and return to the sandpit.

That night he and Ritter had talked until dawn. In the pit, the words sounded less real than dreams, but now their talk was a flushed buck, dressed and cooling. Tomorrow, Ritter had said, Stepan would see Antanas. Dudie and Perchik would change places, and Dudie would be saved. Again—

Perchik's eyes shut. He jammed them open, but slowly they folded. He slid from the stump, his back braced against the bark. The Solingen felt heavy in his hand. He and Ritter would have to remember to search for eggs laid by blowflies in the hair when they quartered the buck at daybreak. Tonight would be cool and in the morning, early, the coolness would still be in the meat . . .

Theo had said he would take one. He would keep Dudie alive. One of them would survive. One only. They all knew. They knew how. They knew why. For Dudie to stay, Perchik had to go. Jakob met death

halfway. Miriam tried to find a way out. But Dudie
. . . with Dudie something went wrong. Dudie they
had agreed to save. He loved Dudie, and Dudie must
live. He'd give anything, even his life. Even twice.
Darkness. Light. Theo. Antanas. Somehow, for Dudie
to live, Perchik must die for him. Was he a bad
brother to wonder. Why?

As he slipped into sleep, Perchik felt Ritter ease the
Solingen and the green arrow from his fingers.

13

IF THE STORM stopped, he might doze. Each time the wind riddled rain across the window, he flinched, certain that a few moments more of darkness, of quiet, of not thinking would tip him into sleep.

Stepan tossed to his side, hiked up his feet—pressing his thighs against his belly—and drew the blanket of stitched rabbit skins over his head.

Choices frightened him. To other people, deciding was easy. Stepan knew what he was *supposed* to do. When there was a problem . . . go in one direction or another. But he couldn't. He couldn't move. He couldn't even run away.

Under the cover the air grew stale. Stepan stretched and with his toes drew down the blanket to his shoulders and tucked it under his chin. The light from the watchtower fronting the railroad spur rolled across the drawn curtain . . . returned . . . rolled . . . returned . . .

Why did he give way when he *knew* what to do? He knew not to answer the knock; he was certain he should not allow Ritter into his room; and after he'd listened, he was sure he shouldn't help. Before the filly he'd been as smart as other people, positive which way to go—but now—this David Fehrmann was a sprung trap.

Ritter said it was simple. Sneak a few bottles—as he had the livers—to Antanas. Ask that Prisoner Fehrmann be given something easier to do than carry railroad ties.

Simple—but Stepan had felt closed in by doubts. Livers . . . schnapps . . . where would it end? Should he hide the schnapps and lie to Ritter, telling him Antanas had said no? But later Ritter might speak to Antanas himself. Why hadn't Stepan been more stubborn and made Ritter himself go with his schnapps to the guard? Why did he have no answer when Ritter said, "Hoegel will protect you"? What if Ritter had been wrong? Who would suffer?

Stepan had been lucky. Antanas made it easy, smiling. What's clinking? Why a brown bag, young man? Where are you going? You're here . . . I'll listen. Tell me. What now?

There was no smile after the boy passed out on the tracks. Antanas had found Stepan—alone, removing the feed bags from the mare and the sorrel—and threatened him. Only later did Stepan understand that Antanas no longer smiled because he no longer heard a clink in a brown paper bag—and that Antanas's meaning was not in the words curdling in his mouth about the anger of the sergeant, but in the craving in his blistered eyes. Unless Ritter found a way to keep washing down the thirst he had reawakened, both David Fehrmann and Stepan would shrivel like Antanas's tongue.

Ritter was unable to make good again on the liquor. Once he started, how would he satisfy Antanas's hunger for deer? Would the deer offer themselves up on a schedule to feed Antanas's appetite? And what would Hoegel do when he found out a Lithuanian guard was dining on venison while he was being supplied by Ritter with hare, creeping with worms and flukes?

The room lit up through the drawn curtains. Thunder rumbled overhead, setting up a yammer among the Alsatians turned loose at night. Stepan pitched to his side and faced the calcimined wall.

Ritter would not be able to lie his way out, not when it came to the Commandant's stomach. Hoegel had been teasing when he'd asked whether Ritter lived alone in the forest or with a lover. Now Ritter said he had not told even Stepan the truth until Stepan had seen his friend, because the boy had escaped from one of the prison trains. Maybe. Maybe Stepan still did not know the whole story. Ritter lied once. Why not again? And why should Stepan protect Ritter if he was a friend, but not—as he thought—his closest friend? If this Fehrmann's brother and Ritter were that important to each other, why did they come to Stepan? He was the outsider. Why was he being pushed into a no man's land between David Fehrmann and Hoegel?

Stepan ran his fingers along the patch of raw flesh where the cheekbone was missing. Maybe he should have teased the filly again. Maybe she'd have kicked harder. The doctor had said, "She almost put you away for good."

Pushing back the rabbit quilt, Stepan rose to his knees and flipped one of the curtains along its rod. With his nail he sprung the front lid on the French hunting watch the Commandant had given him and held it up to the window. Almost four. Lights were not permitted in the barracks for an hour, but if he dressed slowly he could walk to the Commandant's and wait until Hoegel woke.

The wood floor felt wet. Stepan drew on his hopsack trousers and his coarse wool shirt, and sat on the cold hides covering the seat of the Maybach. He untangled his torn socks from the stacked train wheels and slipped them on. Shivering, he blew mists of breath into odd shapes.

If anybody discovered one of the brothers had escaped and was taking the place of the other, the Fehrmanns would push not only Stepan into heavy trouble, but the Commandant as well. Although Hoegel sometimes beat him, he alone never tried to think of new jokes about Stepan's missing cheekbone. At other times he was kind, and he worried about the prisoners. Stepan often heard him on the telephone, shouting into the bad connection, insisting that if he cut rations more, or crowded the laborers, or made examples, the spur never would be finished. Some of the officers snickered that Hoegel's lay-by started no place and made a perfect curve to nowhere. Stepan reported the sneers, and Hoegel told him someday their camp would be important to the war, with trains coming and going; without a lay-by traffic would be very slow. And although Stepan knew he was not smart and did not wear a uniform of whipcord trousers and black

leather boots, he was certain of one thing. The war had
to end, and not go on and on so that every jealous
officer could take his turn as Commandant and prove
that he could do better.

Stepan looked out the window again. The wind had
eased and the drizzle now tumbled in slow drifts. If he
waited here long enough, he would give way again—
not decide anything—and meet Ritter with his venison
as Ritter insisted.

Stepan rubbed the chaff on his shaved head,
stretched, and slid his leather sandals from under the
butcher's block. He unhooked his oilskin from the
nail holding the calendar of the girl on the French
beach, unbolted the door, and stepped into the hover-
ing rain.

The beam on the watchtower cut and recut its arc.
With a strung-out screak, the door closed. Stepan
cringed, but the Alsatians must have roved away in
a pack; not one barked. Drawing the hood—head
down—Stepan followed the whitewashed boulders
along the gravel path toward the Commandant's
caserne.

The guard was not at his post. Under the pergola,
Stepan ran the soles of his sandals over the boot-
scraper. At his touch, the door to Hoegel's bedroom
swung open, and he went in, calling softly: "I'm here
. . . Stepan—"

The pale bulb burned in the fiasco on the Aeolian-
Vocalion phonograph. Hoegel lay naked on the
padded table opposite his Gothic bed, a perfumed
hand towel across his stomach. Crossing to the wood
shelf, Stepan took down the container of French

chalk. As he bent over Hoegel in the dim light, Stepan made out the thin thread, now caked black, splattered in a pool below the ear, and then he saw the small hole in the Commandant's temple.

The door cracked shut and he looked up at a lieutenant he'd never seen, in a uniform with two white lightning flashes on his tight collar, raising a Walther pistol until the muzzle drew level with Stepan's chest. Stepan dropped the container of chalk. Slowly it rolled across the floor. The lieutenant's thumb pressed the safety of the P-38, charging the gun.

I 4

THE OFFICER behind the desk straightened the twin braids of gold on his cap with his gloved hand and said: "The dossier, please."

The corporal rapped his heels together, shifted the Schmeisser to his hip, and opened the top drawer of the metal file cabinet. The officer repeated: "Feldhaber—"

Ritter stood stiffly, only his eyes moving as they scrambled from the officer's glance. He wondered how they could have a file on him. But then, how did they know his name? Out of fear—or caution—he had never told anyone more than, "My name is Ritter." Even with Perchik, who teased him—was Ritter shy because the family tree bore judges, or was he cautious to protect thieves?—Ritter had side-stepped. "If you must have a full name, call me Ritter von Ritterhof." And yet this morning, as Ritter returned from washing in the stream to help Perchik quarter the deer under the spruce, he heard the first call from the bullhorn: "Ritter Feldhaber, report to Commandant Huss . . . Ritter Feldhaber . . . Feldhaber . . . Feldhaber . . . "

Nearer and farther, over and over, setting off yips and caws, fluttering and rustling in the forest. He'd been frightened, but Perchik said he must go, to find out—to find out who was Huss, where was Hoegel— to find out for himself, for Perchik, for Dudie.

At the station platform, 75-mm. self-propelled guns were drawn up, their turrets turned toward the camp, muzzles lowered. Two tanks—one mounting a flame-thrower—flanked the entrance to the compound; and inside, troops, dressed like the officer behind the desk —young, straight, swaggering, with twin lightning flashes glittering in white on their black uniforms— scuffed in heavy boots along the gravel paths. On the apron outside Hoegel's office, a soldier swung an automatic rifle on its forked bipod, aligning his sights in a dry run across his field of fire, and in Hoegel's chair Commander Huss waited, plucking the fingers of the soft kidskin glove tucked into his tunic below the black iron crossbar.

"Have you found it?"

"Here, Commander—"

The drawer of the metal cabinet slid along its glides and slammed shut. The corporal handed Huss a brown folder and stepped back, facing Ritter, one hand resting easily on the barrel, the other on the metal stock of the machine pistol.

"Don't ask for your friends—" Commandant Huss opened the folder. His skin was white in a cap-brim arc to the bridge of his nose and suntanned underneath, and his lips were as thin and taut as sinew. His hair was cut short, and when he bent to read, a bald hoop showed on the top of his head.

"You come from a Bolshevik family."

"I don't understand politics, sir."

Huss looked up. He rubbed his chin with the ring of chased silver on his small finger and examined Ritter's face.

"Pity. Good blood there. Are you the last?"

"I don't know, sir. I hope my mother and father—"

"They're dead."

"Oh—Commandant Hoegel was trying to find them."

"Hoegel's dead."

"I'm sorry, sir."

"Don't be. He was a traitor, too."

"Then there's no one else. I have an uncle, but he's not really an uncle—"

"You had an uncle," Huss corrected.

Huss had not taken his eyes from him. Ritter wished he were alone so he could cry. He turned his face but the corporal holding the Schmeisser waved him back.

Huss said, "I understand, son. And you understand enough, don't you? You understand that politically you present a problem."

"Yes, sir."

Huss closed the dossier.

"You're also aware that we know everything?"

"Yes—"

"Everything."

"Yes, sir."

Huss smiled. "Good stock shows."

"Sir?"

"You agree . . . there are distasteful things that must be done—"

"Yes."

"And comforts—like tears—that are impermissible."

Ritter nodded. Huss turned to the corporal. "Just a child. Alone in the world, but commendable discipline."

The corporal stiffened. "Yes, Commandant."

"Feldhaber," Huss said, still smiling at Ritter. "An appropriate name. Our ancestors, you know, were hewers of wood and drawers of water, at home under an open sky." He held up one gloved and one ungloved hand and stretched his fingers apart. "Self-reliant. Ten fingers and hearts of oak. *Men.*" He leaned forward. "Feldhaber . . . are you too young to enjoy looking under skirts?"

"I know I shouldn't, sir."

Huss laughed. His teeth were capped with gold.

"Oh, but you should, and you must be as bold with women as in your forest."

"Yes, sir."

"Good. Let's work this out, man to man. I'm quite particular. No old hares. No bunnies. I like them plump and tender. Juicy. A female in the third or fourth week—"

"I understand, sir."

"Carry on, as before. Let me see your kill. I'll give you whatever you need."

"The does are in season, sir."

"We'll see." Huss stood. "I expect you to live up to your reputation."

The corporal touched Ritter lightly on the elbow and steered him toward the door.

Huss called across the desk. "Tell me, Feldhaber, are you ever lonely out there?"

"Oh, no, sir."

"You feel no need for companionship?"

"I enjoy being alone, sir."

"Well . . . bring in your bit of fluff and I'll let you sample one of mine."

Ritter crossed the threshold, turned, and saluted. With an exaggerated sweep, Huss lifted his hand to his forehead and said, chuckling, "You'll never want to be alone again."

Huss signaled to the corporal, who swung the door shut with the barrel of the Schmeisser.

15

PERCHIK twisted to his shoulder and tried to make out Ritter's form on the dirt shelf, but they'd plugged their crawl-hole carefully. There was no seepage of light, and the canvas left no vent for their breath. The air was flat, and from its weight on Perchik's chest he guessed daylight might be an hour away.

Ritter's breathing was heavy. Perchik could hear him gulping stale draughts.

The night had been oddly quiet after the rain threat passed. Foxes weren't ferreting or badgers stalking. Only occasionally did a spittle bug whistle or a frog croak.

Ritter coughed and Perchik heard him squirm uneasily.

Perchik whispered: "Ritter—"

Ritter mumbled and began to snore lightly through his open mouth.

Waking Ritter now, pressing him again, would take Perchik no further. Before last night, he'd never seen fear on Ritter's face, and Ritter's fear had alarmed him.

"Didn't you look for Stepan?" he'd asked Ritter.

"Not after Huss warned me."

"Hoegel used to warn you."

"Huss isn't Hoegel."

"You could have passed his barrack."

"I did. The door was open. I didn't see him. Maybe Stepan was there, but I didn't see him."

"Did you see Paulder?"

"I wouldn't know where to look for Paulder."

"Did you ask?"

"Perchik—I was told not to."

"You were right in the camp. You must have heard something. They were all around you. Soldiers talk. Why didn't the prisoners work yesterday?"

"They must have been locked up."

"For Dudie, that would be good."

"Nothing's good, Perchik. Huss is bad. He'll make everything bad."

"Why don't we find out, Ritter? Bring him the venison."

"He asks questions."

"Let him ask."

"How did I kill the deer? With a rabbit trap?"

"Find out about Dudie!"

"Perchik . . . asshead . . . I'm supposed to be out here alone. I tried—"

"But where's Dudie?"

"With the others."

"The others? He's my brother!"

"I did all I could! It's changed! Huss changed everything! Perchik, kill me . . . but I'm not going back. I'm not going back into that camp until I have to. And even then, not without a doe ready to drop her litter on Huss's plate."

Ritter had been sitting at the edge of the pit, breathing heavily. Perchik heard a strange sound, and only after a moment had he fixed on the rasp as coming from the fired-up pull of his own lungs. The two friends—stung—faced each other, an expression on Ritter's face that Perchik had never seen before. Without a word, Ritter slid into the pit. Perchik crossed to the trench stove and struck the holly sticks and screen of woven larch boughs, hiding their cups and pot in the hole under the locust tree and replacing the sod plug. The thunderhead in the west was coming on faster than full night, and after Perchik lowered himself into the pit, he sealed the cover of the crawl-hole carefully. The sound of Ritter's breath was even but controlled. Ritter did not wish to talk. Perchik did, but knew that nothing could be done then. He'd use the night to think, and when they woke, he'd have a plan. When Perchik was sure of himself, Ritter followed always, and he would again. Ritter would have to; nothing they'd ever done had been this important. But Perchik had brooded all night, and although Ritter still was gargling his wet snore on his tongue, soon he would wake—and Perchik did not know what to suggest or to force, or what to do, other than to search their gin traps for a pregnant doe.

Nearby Perchik heard a "ra-ta-tat." Silence, then another short burst of muffled drumming. Perchik thought a woodpecker was out early claiming territory, but a bird called—a musical "tueehh" rather than the woodpecker's shrill "kik"—and Perchik smiled at the picture of a stubborn nuthatch hammering again and again at a tough kernel that wouldn't split.

The "ra-ta-tat" continued—the intervals growing shorter and the spurts longer as the bird pounded away—and then a high-pitched laugh drifted by, as if someone were watching who found the nuthatch and its balky nut more amusing than even Perchik.

Perchik sat up. The laugh turned to a scold, then to a growl: an otter—on its way back to the brook—at bay, facing a threat. As the growl deepened in the otter's throat, a polecat hissed and, with a low bark, struck. The otter screamed. The two bodies thrashed in the underbrush, rolling across the crawl-hole.

Perchik felt Ritter wake and move as the animals whipped about, rumbling and snapping. The cover sagged under the locked, churning bodies, and Perchik wondered what he and Ritter would do if the canvas fell in. The otter whistled. The polecat's claws scratched and dug into the tarp. The otter broke. Chattering, the polecat spun in pursuit. The last flurry was brief. Limping, one body dragged off the other through the scrub.

Perchik set his foot on the dirt shelf holding Ritter's bed and pushed up on the canvas plugging the crawl-hole. The logs and brush had been scattered during the struggle and the tarp lifted easily—but its center fluttered in shreds.

The moon was dim behind a smoke of clouds; in the darkness only a scattering of hoarfrost showed. The thick scent of the polecat hung heavy in the light wind, and as he pulled himself up Perchik's fingers slipped on a rib of blood. Regaining his balance, he sat at the edge of the pit, feet dangling inside.

A low ruffle filtered through the forest, "thrun . . . thrun . . . thrunk . . ."

Wiping off the blood on his worn lederhosen, Perchik said, "Did you hear that?"

From his bed, Ritter answered, "I wasn't sure—"

The thrum rolled in again, overtaken and overlapped by a second run.

Perchik said, "That's not a forest sound."

"To make up for yesterday, maybe Huss is starting the prisoners early."

"Doing what?"

"Maybe he brought new machines to finish the tracks. I saw new tanks."

"Whatever it is—it's near your uncle, not the railroad—"

"Maybe—"

"—but not as far."

"Let Erich Heyler worry."

This time there was a single run, "thrun . . . thrun . . . thrunk . . ." Muddy, flat.

"Is it coming closer?"

"I answered the bullhorns, Perchik."

Perchik shivered, dropped into the pit, and drew on his gray trousers. Holding his stave and arrows, he vaulted through the crawl-hole.

Sprinting, he slid his arm through the sinew sling of the birchbark quiver. He had forgotten to wrap the burlap around his tennis shoes, and they soaked quickly with dew. Soon he was sliding more often than running—making an effort to hold his balance—his face damp with sweat and mist.

"Thrun . . . thrun . . . thrunk . . ."

Again, overlapping. Two runs—or three?

Perchik startled a clutch of birds. Where had they been? He whipped about. Leaves swayed slightly, but the covey was gone. Where? Were they partridge or grouse, or a brood of coot? Had he heard their call? Why couldn't he remember?

He stopped, leaning on the trunk of a young beech, resting his head across his forearm. His temple throbbed against his skin—rapid, thumping. Was he forgetting everything? If Ritter grew numb and he clumsy, neither would be of help; they would drag each other down.

A single "thrunk." A cap to the runs.

Perchik removed an arrow from the quiver and nocked the slot. Bow in one hand, arrow held lightly above the fletching in the other, Perchik moved in a low crouch through the forest.

With a squeak, a shrew broke from its cover of dry grass and shot across his path, jerking and hopping. Horseshoe bats swished and chirped overhead. An engine stuttered and fired, followed by another. Gears ground and meshed. Trucks. Very near—but where? There was no road ahead, not even a trail.

Suddenly, the trucks swung and came up behind him. No, to his left. All around, the forest quivered and rumbled. Frightened, he pressed himself into the knotted branches of a goat willow.

Perchik panted, gulping boosts of air. He felt damp and weak. His hand holding the arrow trembled. Slowly, he stepped clear of the willow. A yellowhammer called sharply, "tyip . . . tyip . . ."

Morning haze sponged up first light. Shadows became shapes. Perchik returned the arrow to the quiver and broke into a run—no longer crouching. Cutting into the breeze chilled him, but before long the forest thinned into a clearing, and at the tree line of a thicket of alder he stopped.

The meadow lay empty. Pairs of crisscrossing tire tracks flattened the grass, except for isolated tufts. Perchik sniffed and peered into the gray light. At the far end of the field a gentle hill bulged, letting off a thick warm cloud—too thick for a drift of manure.

Starting warily along the line of alder, Perchik circled to the gentle swell. As he drew closer, he saw a slip of white. Without searching for movement around the clearing—wondering only a moment where his normal caution had gone—Perchik lifted to a trot, and dropped to his knees beside the mound.

The soil beneath the vapor had been turned over. Clods and loam—cakes of black earth—tumbled in an uneven heap. The slip of white fluttered in the near corner, and when Perchik tugged at the cloth a wrist straightened and a hand—palm up—curled loose. The fingers were bent—the nails clean, buffed . . . feminine.

Perchik set down the stave and tore at the blocks of earth, freeing a swarm of blowflies. Biting, they clustered on his face. He did not brush them away, but continued to claw with both hands, and soon he touched blood still warm, and the soft limpness of a body. After the young woman, he uncovered a middle-aged man—gums clamped as if to hide the shame of his missing bridge—and then scraped clear first the chest; then the shoulder torn away by the bullets; and then the unmarked face of Dudie.

Perchik lifted Dudie free. Brushed off the dirt. Ripped his shirt and covered Dudie's wound.

Perchik slung the sinew of the stave over his shoulder. He carried Dudie into the forest on his forearms and stretched him out beside a fallen limb of hedge elm. Breaking the bough of the elm—the sharp crack ringing through the forest—he dug out a trench with the jagged edge.

Gently, he lowered Dudie into the cut, straightening his legs and crossing his arms on his chest. Perchik removed his prison trousers, stripped off even lengths, shrouded Dudie's bare legs and arms, and wedged rocks over the body to keep out scavengers.

Bending, eyes wet, Perchik kissed Dudie's warm lips.

Dudie had made him cry the first time—Dudie, less than two years old, learning to walk, standing shakily now and then to test his bandy-legged strut. Perchik had been dreaming beside the table, staring into the smoldering cheap candles, weaving fantasies. Dudie wobbled up to him, clutched his leg for support, tried to take another step, and stumbled. As Perchik bent to him, Dudie toppled into the tablecloth, caught his fingers in the worn crochet, and hauled the candelabrum and crystal vase to the floor.

The door jarred open. Jakob stopped, Miriam pressing against his shoulder. She nudged Jakob. He leaned forward but did not move. Miriam reached around and shut the door.

Perchik turned, but Dudie had vanished. Stooping, Perchik saw his brother hidden under the table, gnawing a snuffed candle.

From behind the door, Miriam's whisper came between gasps: "You're the . . . the father."

"An accident can happen to anyone."

"He's old enough . . . to know better. What kind of an . . . an example is he setting for Dudie?"

"Children get into trouble—"

"Trouble. Break . . . breaking things. Why? Jakob . . . why?"

"Why?"

Behind the door it was quiet. Then Perchik heard a deep sigh, and Jakob: "Well . . . yes . . . He is—"

The door opened and Jakob stepped into the room. He kept his hand behind him—on the knob.

Jakob stood before Perchik, waiting for his son to speak. Shifting from one foot to the other—resigned at last that Perchik would remain close-lipped—Jakob made an odd noise in his throat and said, "Perchik, I have something to say to you. Something important. You're old enough, Perchik, to understand. The vase . . . this vase . . . the crystal vase is from your mother's side. You broke . . . Perchik, what I'm trying to say is you broke . . . your mother . . . that is, we planned . . . you broke your wedding present."

Jakob had turned and fled, and Perchik had then, as now, cried.

Perchik brushed back Dudie's hair. He picked off and dropped a tear on Dudie's right eyelid; another on the left. Propping a slab of slate on four stones to clear and shield Dudie's face, Perchik pushed the loose dirt back into the trench. The soil left over he scattered into the underbrush. Hiding the bare patch of earth under a spread of leaves, Perchik turned and walked into the forest without marking the grave.

1 6

RITTER hosed the water through his lips in a thin arcing stream, swallowed the last drops, and said: "There must be others."

He waited for an answer.

"Perchik—"

"Um-m?"

"There must be."

"There must be what, Ritter?"

"Other forests."

"Forests . . ." Perchik waggled his toes in the sunshine. "Where, Ritter?"

"All around. Some might be larger."

"How would we get there?"

"Walk. We'd be safer—"

"Someone would see us."

"Walk at night."

"What would we do there?"

"Same as here."

Perchik's knees tired. He dropped his toes below the water line, filled his lungs with air, and sank. Rolling over, Perchik stroked slowly along the cool muddy bed braided with shingle and rockweed. Lifting his head, he broke water opposite the spit of land jutting into the wallow. The sun was straight up. Ritter continued to float, eyes closed, his body white as chalk.

Ritter ducked back, filled his mouth, and squirted a thin strand of water, trying to hit his bellybutton.

"Perchik—"

Breaststroking, his back warming in the sun, Perchik drew up alongside Ritter.

"Perchik, we have nothing to lose."

A frog appeared on a leaf of arrowhead and rumbled at them.

"You know, Perchik, if the war goes on long enough, the whole whole world might die, and we'd be the only only ones left."

Ritter lifted his head to see whether he was pinwheeling away from Perchik, then dropped back, his long fair hair spreading lazily in the water.

"We'd be able to go anywhere. Find things in empty kitchens to eat. Ham, cheese, wurst, chickens. Live chickens. Cows, even. I bet I could learn to milk a cow. Maybe we'd find a few girls. It would be better with girls."

"Hm-m."

"Wouldn't it?"

"Much better."

"Suppose we find two, and one's ugly and one's pretty?"

"Whoever sees the pretty one first—"

"That's fair."

The frog snorted and pitched into the water.

"It could happen, Perchik."

"Um-m."

"Couldn't it?"

Perchik rolled to his back and floated head to head with Ritter. "It could."

"Even if it doesn't, if everyone doesn't die, the war has to end. Isn't that so?"

Perchik closed his eyes against the sun. "That's so, Ritter."

"What will we do when the war ends?"

"What would you like to do, Ritter?"

"Take a hot bath. Be warm. Every day. Day and night. I remember a tub full of hot water, and then sweating in a bed under a goose-down quilt. In the middle of winter, with snow outside—sweating." Ritter looked toward Perchik. "Did you have a goose-down quilt?"

"Yes, I remember—"

"I'll drink milk," Ritter said. "And juices. Apple. Orange. Grape. With a lot of sugar. And chocolate bars. With nuts. Whole nuts. Did you ever play 'swallow last'? We'll each have a bar, and whoever holds back and swallows the last nut wins. Did you ever play that?"

"No, Ritter."

"I always win."

"Yes, Ritter."

"How will I win?"

Backstroking, Perchik moved away. "However you want."

"However I want what?"

"Hm-n-n?"

Kicking, Ritter raised a welt of foam and pulled up to Perchik. "Are you listening, Perchik?"

"Yes . . . you can have the pretty one."

Ritter flicked his wrist, sprinkling clear beads on Perchik's chin. A brace of coot flew over the wallow, croaking like frogs, their beating wings roughing the water. Banking at the choked point, the match returned, sweeping low over the two floating bodies.

"Will we come back here, Perchik?"

"When?"

"When we're old. First we'll have to go back to school and things like that. Sitting on seats all day wearing tight tight shoes and pants, and shirts with stiff stiff collars and people telling us what to do and I bet even how to talk."

"Um-m-m."

"Maybe we shouldn't leave. Stay away from grown people. No one will find us. What do you think?"

"Yes, Ritter."

"We'll just stay?"

"We'll stay."

Ritter flipped over, treading water easily, and dog-paddled to the bank. He dried himself with his undershirt, drew on his trousers, and sat at the water's edge, rubbing his bare arms briskly. After a few moments, the duck bumps smoothed out and he stopped shivering. Hugging his knees to his chin, Ritter found the sun with his face. He had a thought, and looked toward his friend—yawing in the water, chest puffed. If I go, Ritter thought, I will have to go alone.

When the gnats of light he carried away from the sun stopped sputtering, Ritter said: "No, Perchik. We won't leave Dudie."

Perchik emptied his lungs and sank, without answering, to the bed of the wallow.

17

WHEN RITTER woke, the room was dark, the sky black behind the torn muslin nailed over the window. He touched himself. No clothes, but he felt neither warm nor cold. He hadn't dreamed. He had no memory. He couldn't remember going to bed, or when, or where. He tried to bridge the dead gap, but he was reaching back too far. His uncle would not call soon from the foot of the stairs, and when the moon rose, it would not show in bright pieces behind the tall poplar tree outside his dormer window.

He heard a slight nasal whistle at his side and reached over and touched hair.

Lujza.

Huss's bit of fluff. He was in the camp. A burlap bag leaned against the door filled with sugar, an oil can, salt, tins of army food, a can opener, a loaf of fresh potato bread, a new canvas tarp—and beside him she still slept.

Ritter craned his neck to look at Lujza. The sheet bulged over her hip. Thick black curls tumbled to her shoulders. Her lips parted, and with each whistle Ritter smelled paprika. Her lips were full, the lower heavier and hanging slightly. Ritter's body turned warm.

In a way, he owed this afternoon to Perchik. He had just finished dressing on the bank of the wallow—rubbing warmth into the last of the duck bumps.

"Perchik, the sun's gone gone."

"I can see."

"Aren't you cold?"

"What do you think?"

"You're cold as ice."

Perchik shivered in the water. "You're right, Ritter."

"Then come out."

"Why, Ritter?"

"Why? It's warmer—"

"Why should I be warm, Ritter?"

"Perchik, the moon's got to you."

"Is that bad?"

"Of course."

"How do you know?"

"Everybody knows."

"Everybody knows, Ritter. Everybody knows it's better to be warm. To clean your nails. To be kind. I've been thinking, Ritter—"

Ritter pitched a flat sandstone at Perchik. The stone landed with a slap on his stomach, but Perchik didn't flinch. Ritter said, "You're talking crazy."

"They fooled me. The grown people fooled us."

"I'm going back to the pit, Perchik. I'm hungry."

"Stay dry, Ritter. Say 'Please.' Chew slow—"

"Should I see Huss?"

"Study. Hold the door open for others. Grow up. Grow up like us."

"Should I take a chance and see him?"

"What's so good about grown people?"

"Nothing. But they have the things we want. I think I ought to see him."

Perchik stood up—waist deep—his body peppered with goose pimples. He skipped the sandstone along the wallow's surface. "Why go to Huss?"

"I told you. For supplies."

"What will you take?"

"The venison."

"How did you get venison?"

"I killed a deer."

"With a gin trap?"

"No. I've thought of an answer. I made a bow."

Perchik waded toward the bank with wide-swinging steps. He said, "Go. Don't forget to bring back oil."

After nicking through the glaze with a bone-handled penknife, Huss had sniffed the loin and patted Ritter on the cheek. Breaking into a one-step and rubbing his hands together, Huss said he'd learned more about Feldhaber from seeing him—from his pure blue eyes and straight fair hair—than from his dossier. Huss called Ritter "Thor" and asked the corporal holding the Schmeisser if he had to make a bow, could he tell a yew tree from a fence post? Huss asked Ritter what he used for arrows, and when Ritter answered "ash," Huss bent over and whispered that venison was not a doe ready to drop, but Huss would stretch a point for a hewer of wood and slayer of beasts. Huss winked to the corporal, who led Ritter out into the sunlight and to a side barrack.

Ritter hesitated on the threshold. The corporal nudged him into the room—dim, its lone small window covered with a tatter of muslin. Ritter held back, pressing against the muzzle of the Schmeisser. The corporal prodded Ritter and whispered, "In a few hours I'll send the Engineers to pry you loose," and shut the door.

When Ritter opened his eyes again, a small bulb, dangling from a loose wire, had been turned on. Lujza was smoking a cigarette of raw tobacco rolled in newspaper. She had put on a thin red dress strewn with enormous yellow flowers, and Ritter wasn't sure how —but he was certain she wore nothing underneath.

Lujza smiled and crossed to the narrow bed and leaned over and kissed Ritter on the lips. He gagged at the rush of smoke and paprika, but his hand reached out, without his willing it. Lujza laughed and held his wrist. She was strong and drew his hand away from the moistness under her dress.

"Another time."

"When?"

She smiled. Her left eyetooth was missing. "When I let you."

Lujza released him. His fingers smelled of fresh mint. She said, "You tell Huss—how it was, and that you want to come back."

"I'll tell him I love you."

"Me? You love one part and don't even know its name. But you'll be good. You're full of juice. Get some practice, and you can stay the night—"

"I have no one to practice with."

"Where do you live?"

"In the woods."

"Ah-h. You'll find someone. When it's still new, it's

best under the sky. You think the whole world's looking, but it isn't."

"Suppose—"

"Suppose—" She shrugged and showed the gap in her teeth. "Once, someone was peeping. Has it harmed me?"

"Oh, no—"

Lujza crossed to a porcelain basin on a three-legged table propped against the wall. She soaked the end of a towel and brought it to him.

"Cool your jigger off—"

He didn't understand. Lujza reached for the sheet but suddenly Ritter felt shy and clutched the edge. She grinned and dropped the wet towel on the bump.

"Don't worry, he'll rise again. He's learned his manners." She pinched Ritter's cheek. "Whenever a lady comes into the room, he'll stand."

She sat at the edge of the bed. Ritter swabbed himself under the sheet. "If you like the woods, I live there," he said.

"For me, that's too long ago—"

"Can I bring someone here?"

"Who?"

"A friend."

"From the woods?"

"Oh, no! Just someone . . . someone I like. You'll like him, too."

"How old?"

Ritter hesitated. "Almost as old as me."

Lujza laughed. She pulled down the sheet and studied Ritter a moment, the tip of her tongue probing the gap in her teeth.

"Let me see him. If he has enough beef . . . you can ask the Commandant."

Ritter said, "Thank you," and as he dressed, Lujza bent her head—her thick black curls touching the floor —brushing her hair vigorously with an old bristle brush.

At the door, Ritter knotted and lifted the burlap bag. He turned. Lujza, grunting with each stroke, did not look up, and he left without a word.

The light from the watchtower rolled across the fields and trees facing the camp—and returned. Thunder rumbled in the distance but the sky was clear. Ritter filled his lungs with cool evening air, let out a cloud of frost smoke, and closed his eyes. How could he explain to Perchik? How would he describe Lujza? How could he share? They would. They shared everything. Ritter couldn't bring Perchik into the camp. Lujza wouldn't go to the pit.

He'd leave the solution to Perchik. Perchik was smart. Perchik would find a way.

1 8

SITTING on his wood slab with his feet crossed under him—plucking at the edge of his sock where his elf toe poked through—Ritter had said: "There was nothing. I didn't even feel Lujza beside me. When I fell asleep, everything ended. No dreams. Nothing. If I slept like that at night, a boar could fall on me."

Perchik reached across the pit with his yew stave and flipped Ritter's shag of hair.

"A wild boar?"

"I'm serious, Perchik."

"You wouldn't feel *any*thing?"

"Nothing."

"A full-grown wild boar?"

Ritter warned, "Perchik—"

Perchik nudged Ritter under the arm with the stave.

"The boar might stick you awake—"

Ritter held the tip of the stave and leaned forward. "I didn't feel, asshead. I didn't hear. I forgot everything. I woke up thinking I fell asleep years ago."

Perchik studied Ritter. For sure, the Gypsy had worked some magic on him.

Perchik said, "Then what?"

"Then I wanted her again."

"Again?"

Ritter released the stave. "Again, asshead. That's all you think about."

"All?"

"All."

"Food . . ."

"I don't want food. I want Lujza."

"A tub full of hot water."

"I want her to touch me."

"Your uncle . . ."

"Asshead. You still don't understand."

Ritter scraped away at dirt covering his large toe, then lifted his head and said: "Perchik, if I had to pick between never seeing you again or her again—I'd see Lujza."

Perchik looked surprised.

"That much?"

"Perchik—you'll feel the same."

"Hm-n . . ."

Ritter shut his eyes, remembering.

"Perchik, how do we put you with Lujza?"

"Well—"

"Yes?"

"I think you were right yesterday. We ought to get out of here. Anywhere. Away from the camp. To another forest. Any forest—"

Ritter had tumbled to his back, laughing, holding his belly, then clasping both hands over his crotch. "Perchik, I love it, I love it, I love it. You will, you will, will, will."

Ritter had straightened his legs, still holding himself, and, smiling, had fallen asleep.

His breathing had been deep and even. He didn't

stir at the snap and roll of the thunderhead to the east. Perchik lay awake—waiting—but the rain hadn't come and the storm passed them by.

Perchik tried to put Lujza together. Dark hair, darker eyes. Lips—the bottom straight, the upper bowed. Voice smoky. She would smell of damp leaves steaming in sunshine. Breasts large, but without bounce.

When the women lined up on the railroad platform, Perchik had noticed that young breasts didn't droop. What held them up? Were young breasts hard, and old soft and runny? Would a hard breast be more pleasant to touch?

Perchik heard a sharp scratch. Had it come from inside their pit? He'd warned Ritter that just the smell of fat drew rats, and he wondered whether Ritter had brought in food or forgotten to wash his hands.

Ritter now had a night's puddle of spit in his mouth. Over his gargling and choking, Perchik thought he heard the scrape again.

The dense air told him they'd passed more than half the night. Perchik was tired but couldn't sleep, gorged with scraps of venison but hungry, and most of all—even with Ritter beside him—suddenly lonely. His chest pinched as Jakob came through the dirt wall, his hand behind him holding tight to a doorknob. Under the table, Dudie—with toothless gums—gnawed at the snuffed candle. Soon Jakob would shift from one foot to the other, and the strange sounds he heard were not someone named Ritter but his father clearing his throat.

"Poppa—I'm listening. Come. Closer. You can touch me. No one's looking—"

Ritter gagged and tossed to his side.

Perchik sat on his wood slab and reached for his bow and quiver.

Pushing up on the new canvas, Perchik uncovered the crawl-hole. He wriggled through the narrow opening and closed Ritter in under the tarp and a scatter of leaves.

The air nipped. Softly the stream tumbled along its banks. A spittle bug whistled under a shrike's scold.

Perchik paced off the few steps to the trench stove and in the dark ran his fingers along the slab. He felt the cold metal of the gin trap that again had broken its spring.

Ritter had wanted to leave and now wished to stay. Perchik, who had been certain they must stay, felt like running. He no longer belonged in the pit or in these woods. But if not here—where?

Perchik crossed to the locust tree that held their cache of sugar and looked up at the birch basket covered with netting.

He would walk, not sneak in; in daylight, straight across the compound, not at night in shadows. Push open Lujza's door. Let her make him forget. Everyone. Ritter, Jakob and Miriam, Dudie. Let her do it to him once. Then turn to face the soldiers as they broke in, machine pistols cocked. He'd laugh at them, because he'd be done—with everything.

Perchik walked to the bank. The water picked up and tossed shreds of moonlight downstream. The bed was full and the lurching brook flushed over into shallow sloughs. A dipper roving the stream bed—feeding underwater—rose to the surface, flicked its feathers and stub tail, and returned to its rock perch. Stretching out on the bank, Perchik ducked his head into the water.

The cold shocked his cheeks numb. He let out a thin stream of bubbles and pressed lower. With a roar, water tumbled into his ears. He opened his eyes. As dark as the pit.

Perchik felt blood rushing to his head. His lungs grubbed for air.

He pushed down farther.

He would never sleep again. Never dream. Never wake up thinking about Lujza, wondering whether he, too, would prefer Lujza to Ritter . . .

Never.

Perchik's head bobbed up.

Gasping, he fell on his back. He was angry. He hadn't meant to come up, hadn't said to himself find air.

Perchik sat. Seeds of light swirled before his eyes. At first he thought they were fireflies, but as the blood left his temples and his breathing evened, the specks slipped away.

Perchik rubbed his forehead, warming with the tingle.

The seeds reappeared. They did not quiver. They were far, not close; not fireflies, or the first muddled vision after hanging upside down in a stream. The lights were not part of his forest. They were held by men.

Perchik rose, holding his yew stave, the quiver slung over his shoulder, and leaned into a steady lope. He ran straight, scattering shrews and hamsters underfoot, dodging tree trunks and leaping fallen bracken as he cut a path toward the pinpoints. For fear of circling in the dark, he dropped into ravines—sliding down scarps and scrambling up far bluffs—avoiding easy half-turns around level rims. As Perchik broke over the lip of each rake, he saw the lights still straight on— no larger—not moving now, and although he was plunging toward a corner of the forest far from the mound in the meadow, soon he heard the first "thrun . . . thrun . . . thrunk . . ."

The lights wouldn't come nearer. Were they on the Rhine? Jamming air into his lungs, Perchik opened his mouth. His breathing and gasping grated in the quiet night. He began to slide on patches of dew and felt his gait grow choppy, his pace jerky.

"Thrun . . . thrun . . . thrunk . . ."

His right foot came down on air. Perchik lurched and felt his ankle turn under him as his heel scraped the skirt of a pothole. He fell heavily, ramming his temple into the ground to protect the quiver of arrows. He lay on his side stunned, for a moment aware only of the seep of blood under his eye, trickling over his lips to his chin.

Nearby a lapwing called through its nose: "vee-veet." A long-eared owl, its ear tufts erect, sat on the crown of an alder looking straight down at him. Near the owl's head, the moon lost its lower turn to a scrap of cloud.

Perchik gave in to the weariness from the run. The night's sleeplessness smothered him. His lungs stopped sponging air, and as his lids settled he winced with the first thrust of pain from his ankle.

He opened his eyes and sat. Leaning on his left foot,

he stood. Ahead the lights were clearer, in sets—not moving—and then one pair went out.

Dragging his leg, feeling the pain split up his side when his weight came down on his right ankle, he limped forward.

Perchik heard an engine turn over and the chug and pop of a muffler. Two lights moved. He started to run, sweating for the first time—the chilled sweat of pain and fear.

"Thrun . . . thrun . . . thrunk . . ."

Then—a single "thrunk."

He almost stumbled into the open meadow—as hidden as the mound in the field ringed by alder. A tractor, its skip loader lifted, swayed and dipped along a set of tire tracks pressed flat in the tall grass. Under the high-beam lights of a six-wheel Henschel, a new hill bulged, oozing vapor. A figure bent low to the ground. A pistol fired. "Thunk." The officer—twin lightning flashes glittering on his black uniform—straightened and sheathed his Luger.

Perchik dropped to his left knee and lifted his right. Reaching for an arrow, he felt for the cock feather and nocked the butt. Canting the bow, he drew, anchored on his cheekbone, sighted—and loosed.

The arrow arched smoothly and struck the officer in the neck as he stepped forward, just below the Adam's apple.

1 9

RITTER sat and tried to fill the dead gap. For a moment he did not know where he was. With Lujza? In the pit? The pit . . . Since he'd been with the Gypsy, his senses went to sleep with him. The pit was not a barrack. Sleeping like a dormouse was a risk.

Perchik shouldn't have let him sleep late. The rapid call of a swooping goshawk had replaced the night chirp of the bat, and as he listened Ritter thought the "yer-rik" was too close—Perchik teasing again—but the second grunt came clearly from the wallow.

Morning was in full flush over the tarp. Ritter studied the pattern of brush covering the canvas. Fingers . . . No, her web of black . . . guided by Lujza—lower and lower . . . touching her . . .

Ritter stood on the dirt shelf that held his slab bed and pushed through the crawl-hole.

The grass fringing the pit was almost dry. The sky was fresh, the sun strong. Ritter breathed deeply. Pine, musk, resin—but no woodsmoke.

Perchik had not fired the kindling they'd left under the rock slab in the trench stove. Ritter dropped the fuzz sticks in place, unhooked the canteen, and went for water.

On the bank, Perchik—leaning on his yew stave—

had left fresh marks. Perchik was not stoking the trench stove, bringing down stores from the locust tree, washing—but a limb of buckthorn hung, split at the bole. Odd. Perchik had run straight through it.

Ritter followed the trail into the wood. Baffled, he read Perchik's spoor: spurning open pockets, plunging head-on into thickets, sliding into muddy sinks. Soon Ritter realized Perchik was not tracking. Game did not plunge headlong, except in short bursts.

Clumsily, Perchik had left tracks a squirrel could follow at night. Perchik—who wouldn't leave their camp before he'd scattered brush along the edge of the smoke screen to break the straight line. Ritter didn't understand. Was Perchik frightened? Had he panicked? Was he fleeing?

Ritter stopped and bent low over a patch of loam in the shade of a laurel. The press of the burlap covering Perchik's tennis shoes showed clear—one heavier than the other. Perchik was sparing his right foot. Had someone—something—hurt him?

Slowly, Ritter circled—moving farther to the right and to the left—lifting chickweed and spurge, and studying moss, ground, and grit underneath.

Ritter turned back to the laurel, puzzling over Perchik's clear mark in the clay—when the first bay of an Alsatian swept in, followed by an answering chorus of howls: shrill, straining, savage.

Ritter folded. He sat on the ground, his body shaking.

Was he now alone?

The yelping echoed. Moved. Seemed closer. To the side.

On hands and knees, Ritter scuttled into the cover of a low-spreading maple. He crimped his back against the trunk, and the broad leaves and brown buds fell back into place in front of him.

Ritter heard only his own heavy panting. He filled his lungs and held his breath. He thought he caught one last yip and strained forward. Nearby, field mice skittered about in creepers and a pair of hazel hens took turns whistling.

Time slipped by. He hadn't dozed, or dreamed, or daydreamed. He hadn't heard or seen or felt, and yet the coolness told him hours had passed and shadows were flattening.

Ritter crawled out and stood. The sun had hardened Perchik's tracks in the loam into a ribbed pattern, splayed in the center by the forepaw of a passing hedgehog. Heavy clouds milled overhead. Evening would be cool.

Ritter looked over his shoulder. Perchik had traveled in a beeline. Glancing down occasionally for Perchik's signs, Ritter tracked, hoping the trail would lead to a grove of ripe white pears, to a gin trap Ritter had forgotten, or to Perchik himself—grinning at his cleverness in frightening Ritter.

Ripe, top-heavy meadow grass bent in the still air under its own weight, razed by crisscrossing sets of tire tracks. At the far end of the field a patch swelled. Black. Earth turned up drew a dark hive, the hungry buzz drilling into Ritter.

He looked away, nestling his chin in his shoulder. Dudie . . . Stepan . . . Hoegel . . .

Had they found Perchik?

He'd never go back to Huss. Never see Lujza. He'd never . . .

What would he do?

He was alone. What could he do alone? Perchik was the hunter. Perchik . . .

First, he heard the echo.

Whoever was speaking, swung the bullhorn.

". . . hearing . . ."

The sound was muffled, crackling with static.

". . . haber . . . the Commandant . . ."

The voice moved closer. Ritter heard, ". . . your age . . ." Again, he was certain as he strained, ". . . a fair hearing . . ." and then—"Feldhaber."

The words garbled, drifting away, but soon swung back, coming toward him . . . and underneath—muzzled at first—the shrill whining of the Alsatians filtered through.

Ritter ran.

He ran like Perchik. Straight. Through shrubs. Tumbling into draws and scrambling out—nails hooking into sod. Hearing only the ". . . Feldhaber . . ." and the savage straining of the dogs. Sweating. Smelling the blood beginning to drain from the cross-cuts on his face laid open by thorns and thistle.

Ahead, the brook pitched over a clog of rock. Ritter turned at the plunging water—and stopped.

His mouth open—panting—he shook his head to clear the throb of blood in his ears.

The dogs were no closer—but no farther. He'd run as fast as he could. How many Alsatians were there? Was he running away from one pack and into another? Did it matter where he ran, since sooner or later they'd cut his trail?

His trail.

Asshead—

At the edge of the stream Ritter slipped out of his hobnailed boots and knotted the laces. He removed his socks and stuffed them into the right boot. His trousers rolled up—the boots strung over his neck—he stepped into the rush of water.

Ritter walked downstream, picking his way—careful not to turn over rock or shingle—and was upon it before he saw the sudden movement in the yellow spikes of the blooming water-pepper.

2 0

THE SHAGGY MAPLE hugged the brook beside the water-pepper, and in their adjoining notches neither Ritter nor Perchik had been able to sleep. Most of the troops had left, but now and then a soldier tromped through the brush behind an Alsatian, flash-light bobbing as though it were riding the roll of the stream.

Ritter leaned over toward Perchik, tucked into the elbow formed by the trunk and a low bough whose leaves touched water.

"Perchik?"

"Whisper!"

"Perchik—"

"Yes?"

"Will they go away?"

"They'll go away, Ritter."

"How do you know?"

"We didn't leave any track."

"How long can we walk in the stream?"

"As long as we have to."

A light seesawed toward them. Underbrush snapped and a dog growled.

Perchik said, "They'll get tired before us. Shh . . ."

On the bank, a soldier—dressed in black, with the

twin lightning flashes on his collar—played the beam of his flashlight along the timber line facing him. The light swung and probed the crown of the maple over them. Ritter moaned with fear. Perchik held up his hand reassuringly. The beam slid to the water-pepper, skipped back to the maple, and then danced downstream and snapped off.

The soldier slacked his leash. The Alsatian bent to the water and drank, slopping noisily. The dog lifted and turned its head, but braced its paws against the soldier's tug.

Laughing, the soldier leaned over, unsnapped the leash from the choke-chain, and said, "All right. Go, Hansie—"

The Alsatian breasted into the brook. Quickly, its legs were lifted off the stream bed. Stroking strongly, the dog swung into the rapids, paddling in place against the rush of white water.

Neatly the soldier stacked his flashlight, leash, and K-43 rifle. Sitting on the bank, he unlaced his boots, peeled off his socks, cuffed his whipcord trousers, and thrust his feet into the stream. With a shocked "Ac-c-ch!" he jerked them back, then—with pauses—forced his toes into the freezing water.

Only the nose, eyes, and ears of its head showing, the Alsatian began to move forward, gaining speed, cutting the stream in half and sending eddies to both banks. The soldier flipped a dried clog of willow into the water. The dog's head turned at the splash. With a low whistle, the soldier pointed to the bobbing stick. The dog sprinted and clamped the stick between its jaws.

The dog remained in midstream.

"Hansie—*come!*"

The Alsatian stiffened its tail but hesitated. The soldier stood and showed the leash. Thrusting its head forward, the dog swam to the bank and released the stick at the soldier's feet.

He bent and leashed the Alsatian and said, "Good Hansie." The dog shook—head to tail and back—clearing its coat and showering the soldier.

The soldier said, "Hansie, monster," but he was smiling. He drew on his socks and boots, and snapped on the flashlight. Idly, he ran the beam along the opposite bank—panning slowly—stopping at the maple.

Ritter whispered, "Go away. Please, please go away!"

The light hung in their eyes. Perchik slid an arrow from his quiver. Ritter reached over and gripped the bow, pressing the string and stave together. Angrily, Perchik tried to shake the bow loose, raking the lobed leaves overhead.

Ritter held on.

The light went out.

When their eyes adjusted again to the darkness, Ritter said, "Did he go away?"

"He went away, Ritter."

Perchik settled into the elbow of the maple.

Ritter hugged himself for warmth and said, "I'm hungry."

"Soon we'll leave."

"How soon?"

"With the light."

"They'll be back—" Ritter rubbed his thighs with his palms and said, "Won't they?"

"They'll keep looking—"

"Perchik?"

"Yes."

"Every time a dog picks up your track, the soldiers think it's me."

"Good. The more they're mixed up, the better."

"Perchik, they're not mixed up. To them all the tracks are mine. They don't know about you."

Beneath them a drifting badger popped up, snorting in pleasure.

"Perchik?"

"Yes, Ritter."

"Tell me again."

"I didn't think."

"Nothing?"

"I didn't stop—"

"How could you not think?"

"I just did it."

"But you knew it wouldn't be you, it would be me—"

The badger waddled to the shore, rooted about, and dived back into the brook.

"They're looking for me, Perchik. I killed him."

"I'm sorry."

"Sorry—"

"For you, not for the officer."

Perchik drew away from the jagged bark, shifting his lean from his left to his right shoulder.

Ritter said, "What will they do with me?"

"We'll be together. Whatever they do with me."

A gray bird fluttered to a limb below them and called several times: "cu-khoo . . . cu-khoo . . ." Her mate babbled in quick answer and the cuckoo flew off.

Ritter said, "There's light in the sky."

"Not yet. We need to see. Not too much. On the ground. Enough not to make mistakes."

Suddenly—behind them—a dogfight broke out: snarling and snapping; scrub and brush scattering. Held apart by two exhorting soldiers, straining on hind feet, front legs pawing at each other, jaws inches apart, two Alsatians boiled out of a thicket along the bank. Choke-chains bit into their throats, tongues rolled to the side, pink lips dribbled. A third dog appeared—snubbed short on a leash by a corporal—stepping guardedly, its hackles stiff, caught up in the frenzy. The corporal—squat and solid—waved his hand and called out. The two soldiers pulled their dogs apart, each arguing that his Alsatian would be the stronger stud—turning to the corporal, who said if they'd been let loose they'd have mangled each other to death . . . neither deserved a sniff of his bitch.

The soldiers straggled along the stream, turned a bend, and soon Ritter and Perchik heard them crossing the brook at a narrow waist. Loud laughter, a flat smack in water, splashing—and a gray cap floated downstream, followed by the stocky corporal, knee high, making one last lunge, his fingers touching but not holding the cap. The corporal spat and sloshed back. The cap rode past the water-pepper, soaking up and growing heavy with water, and sank.

Gradually, the voices of the soldiers faded.

Perchik touched Ritter lightly with the yew stave. "In a few minutes—"

Pitch drained from the sky. Top shoots of trees

showed against a rim of light blue. Single calls and skitterings grew louder . . . drew answers . . . overlapped. On the ground, shadows drew back from boulders and hedges and straightened into silhouettes.

Perchik stretched. His lips twitched and his body quivered against the chill air. He let the spasm run its course, gripped the bough under him, and swung to the ground.

Perchik removed the burlap and sneakers. Ritter dropped to his side, the hobnailed boots in a yoke around his neck.

Perchik stepped into the stream. The brook felt cold only at the water line—a blade of ice cutting his thighs. Very slowly, stopping to listen every few steps over the gurgle—Ritter to his side and slightly behind —Perchik waded along the shelf where the bank of the stream bottomed out.

They passed the waist, upstream of the bend—the soldiers' crossing. A string of white rock bridged the brook, except for the cobble that had tipped the stocky corporal over, which listed, muddy underside up.

The shelf narrowed, the flow of the stream quickened, and ahead lay a stretch of churning, foaming river—deep, cutting bluffs straight up and down out of both banks.

Perchik stopped.

At his side, Ritter whispered, "Should we swim?"

"No."

"We'll leave a trail—"

"We can't—"

"Perchik, either you . . ."

A scream sent coveys and broods of birds swarming.

Leaning forward, digging their hands into the water like oars, Perchik and Ritter raced for the cover of the bank and huddled against each other.

A whine. A pathetic bark. A yelp of pain.

Ritter looked about—found his bearings—and pointed: "Our gin trap—"

The current bearing him, Perchik plunged downstream—almost toppling face forward—to a footing in the bluff and scaled the drop. Crouching, he sprinted up the slope to a shock of tower mustard, cut through a reach of ribbon grass, and dropped to his knees behind a thick larch.

Ahead, an Alsatian tugged at a rear paw clamped in steel jaw-pillars, feebly dragging the baseplate along the ground. The squat, solid corporal stood over his bitch, a Luger hanging heavily in his right hand. With an effort, the corporal lifted the muzzle and placed it in the dog's ear and fired.

Perchik nocked an arrow.

The soldier bent over.

Again, the Luger cracked, bucking the corporal's arm. He holstered the pistol, stepped over the dog, and gripped the anchoring steel stakes.

Perchik drew.

Ritter, running up behind, leaped for the bow. Twisting his shoulders, Perchik threw Ritter—and loosed.

The arrow wobbled, and as the corporal straightened to face them, struck him low—sideslipping—above the groin.

Head down, Ritter plunged again. Perchik buckled

under his weight, the birchbark quiver falling free. Sobbing, stifling a moan in his throat, Ritter lunged for the stave. Perchik pried it loose. Perchik rolled over, face down—outstretched hand holding the bow —Ritter sitting the small of his back, grinding his knee into Perchik's elbow. Perchik heaved. Ritter rode him, coming down heavily, driving the air from Perchik's chest. With his free left hand, Perchik reached for an arrow and jammed the pile into Ritter's bare thigh.

Ritter choked off a gasp of pain. Blood bubbled. Ritter snapped up a shard of traprock and pounded down on Perchik's fingers.

Bone cracked.

Perchik's hand clutching the bow cramped; went limp.

Bent double, the corporal stumbled toward them, the arrow in his left hand, his right groping for the Luger, dragging entrails from the hack above his crotch where he'd pulled the point free.

The corporal spread his legs, coughed once—and softened to the ground.

Ritter turned.

Perchik was on his back. The fingers of his right hand looked funny. Broken twigs.

Ritter knew something terrible had happened and wanted to look up into Perchik's face, but couldn't.

WHEN THEY reached the bank near the pit, Ritter thought Perchik would faint again. The strips of burlap holding the wood splints were wet and loose, the rubbing of the sling had blazed a red blister across his neck, and Perchik had gnawed a gash into his lower lip smothering the ache.

Ritter reached down to help Perchik from the stream. Perchik, the water rippling around his hips, did not move.

Ritter said, "Closer—"

Perchik dipped his face into the brook, wiped the blood from his chin, and held out his left hand. Ritter locked Perchik's wrist in his grip and strained. Perchik braced against the shelf, slithered in the mud, then fell forward on his left side. Ritter slipped his hand under Perchik's knee and drew him over the edge of the bank.

Perchik sprawled on his back.

Ritter said, "The splints are loose—"

In the distance the bullhorns repeated—over and over—the last, the very last warning to Ritter Feldhaber to give himself up.

Perchik lifted his elbows. Gripping Perchik under the armpits, Ritter propped him to a sitting position in the shade of a birch. Perchik shifted into the light.

"Maybe the sun will dry the burlap tight," he said.

Taking cover behind the trunk, Ritter looked toward the pit, waving off a hive of aphids. Ritter said, "I don't see anyone."

"Why should you?"

"If he's near the pit, I'd see him."

"You might . . ." Perchik plucked a wad of grass and wedged it between the blister and the sling. ". . . you might not."

"You mean if he's there, he's hiding."

"That's what I would do."

"Perchik, there's the locust tree and our basket. I could be back in a few minutes."

Perchik shook his head. Ritter bent, picked up a stone, and hefted it.

"Suppose I throw a rock?"

"Suppose you do."

"If there's an Alsatian, he'll bark."

"They're trained, Ritter. They bark when they're supposed to. They attack when they're told to. They follow trails they're led to, and our tracks are all over. If the soldiers found the pit, one of them is there, hiding like a coward—"

"I'm going."

"—waiting for you to prove Huss is right. You're a true Feldhaber—"

Ritter rolled down his pants, shucked the strung boots off his neck, and moved past the trunk.

Perchik said, "The soldier will kill you."

Ritter stopped and turned. Twice he started to say something, then blurted: "Do you care?"

"Asshead—"

"Why do you?"

"You're my friend."

"There's another reason, Perchik."

"Tell me."

"You need someone."

"I'd do better without you."

Dropping and nudging the rock along the ground with his toe, Ritter returned to the birch and stood over Perchik.

"Perchik—"

"Yes?"

"What should we do now?"

"Keep going."

"I'm hungry, Perchik."

"We'll find something."

Perchik held up his arm and Ritter drew him to his feet. Waggling his left hand between the stave and the string, Perchik slid the bow to his shoulder beside the quiver. He spread the bunched-up burlap sling along his right forearm and said, "You first, then help me down."

Ritter jumped into the brook. Perchik leaned on him lightly and eased down the bluff.

They moved upstream, close to the bank, seeking shade and cover in their loop around the open wallow, not reaching the stream flowing in until the shank of the afternoon.

Above the wallow they branched off into a fork they could not remember ever having followed. The feeder was narrower than the stream but deeper and swifter, and at the foot of a falls they found watercress and turnips. They ate the watercress and leafy tops of the turnips, and saved the roots.

The falls topped out into a pure stand of pine, the ground deep with layered cones and needles. The air was full of strange twittering and chittering, and a brace of deer wallowing in mud faced down the two intruders—unafraid of the unfamiliar.

At last Perchik urged Ritter forward, and the hind and his doe pranced off.

Beyond the mudhole, the bed of the fork grew shallow and wide, and split around an oval-shaped flat.

Perchik pointed to the island ahead, and sifted the shallow bed until he found two sharp-edged slates. He told Ritter to gather up fallen fern—broad-leaved, if possible—and then led the way to the mud bar.

Seepage was light as they dug—the walls held firm —and by nightfall they'd scooped out a tight trench, breaking up the clods and scattering the sludge in the stream.

They ate the turnip roots, spread dry broom in their cut, lay down side by side, and pulled the green fern over their faces.

Neither slept.

The stream flowed soothingly around the oval-shaped bar, but through the thick screen of leaves they could not see whether the night was clear or overcast.

In fits and starts, they dozed; Ritter snoring, Perchik moaning with pain.

Ritter shook off a bad dream. He couldn't remember what had frightened him. Something ugly—hairy —and the noise had been part of the nightmare.

But he was awake.

Beside him, he felt movement.

And the sound . . . grating.

Engines, close by. Gears. Trucks.

"Perchik—"

Wood rattled in the quiver, and a corner of the screen lifted. Soft light folded in.

"Perchik, you can't shoot with broken fingers."

Perchik shifted awkwardly in the trench. Ritter said, "I won't let you."

Perchik twisted about and rose to his knees. Ritter whispered, "If you stop, they'll think we ran away."

Holding the stave in his left hand, Perchik stooped out of the trench. Screaming *"I won't let you!"* Ritter jolted to his feet—scattering the cover of fern—and pounced on Perchik's bent back.

Ritter pinned Perchik's arms to his side. The bow clattered to the ground. With his left elbow, Perchik slammed at Ritter's groin—missing—ripping him low in the stomach. Ritter hawked air, but held his grip.

The engines cut out.

Silence.

Then, a salvo.

"Thrun . . . thrun . . . thrun . . . thrunk . . ."

Perchik pitched and plunged wildly, kicking with his heels. Ritter felt his shin sear, lost his balance, and fell heavily on his back—Perchik crashing into his chest.

Arrows scattered from the quiver.

Perchik screamed at the race of pain in his broken fingers.

They lay, both whimpering—face up, Perchik on

top of Ritter, his fingers locked on Ritter's arm gripping his chest.

"Thrun . . . thrunk . . ."

Perchik whipped his face forward, closed his teeth on Ritter's thumb, and bit. Ritter gagged on a sob. Perchik tasted salt and blood. Ritter jerked his hand, tearing loose, sliding his freed arm up—hooking Perchik under the chin—then heaving and pitching both of them over.

Perchik stretched out flat, face down, under Ritter.

Ritter tightened his grip on Perchik's head. Perchik gasped, tried to say something, bucked once, and then yielded.

Ritter's breathing grew even. Perchik seemed asleep. Ritter eased his hold on Perchik's neck, and wondered whether Perchik had begun to babble in a dream, until he looked up.

An officer in a black uniform—knee-length boots brightly polished, holding a huge Alsatian in check—stood at the brink of the shallow bed, hailing Ritter.

Ritter looked down.

"Perchik—"

Ritter nudged Perchik.

"Wake up—"

Perchik's head thudded to the ground.

Ritter shook him. "Are you all right?"

Perchik's head rolled. His wrist and broken fingers were bent under his chest. He should have been screaming in pain, but only stared at a switch of fern.

Ritter heard the splash. The Alsatian, yowling widely, raked the officer into the water. The officer jerked the leash, shifted it to his left hand, and unbuckled the holster. Ritter picked up the bow and scrambled for an arrow. The officer leveled his Mauser. Without sighting—drawing flat and level—Ritter loosed. The pile punched into the officer's chest.

The Alsatian broke free. Quickly Ritter nocked another arrow and loosed. Too high.

Head low, the dog splashed across the shallow stream. Ritter grasped, and felt his fingers close around the point. He slid his hand along the length of ash toward the nock end, but as his fingers reached the cock feather, fangs loomed. Ritter fell on Perchik, spreading lengthwise over his body, his cheek pressed against Perchik's.

The sun was soft on Ritter's neck. He brushed off an ant crawling across Perchik's open eye and whispered, "Perchik, quick—"

The first crunch—in the shoulder—stung, but then the jaws closed over his throat and Ritter knew Perchik couldn't hurry, and he wouldn't have to wait long for death to cover the pain.

A NOTE ON THE TYPE

This book was set on the Linotype in Granjon, a type named
in compliment to Robert Granjon, but neither a copy of
a classic face nor an entirely original creation. George W.
Jones based his designs for this type on that used by
Claude Garamond (1510–61) in his beautiful French books,
and Granjon more closely resembles Garamond's own
type than do any of the various modern types
that bear his name.

Robert Granjon began his career as typecutter in 1523.
The boldest and most original designer of his time, he
was one of the first to practice the trade of typefounder
apart from that of printer. Between 1557 and 1562 Granjon
printed about twenty books in types designed by himself,
following, after the fashion, the cursive handwriting of
the time. These types, usually known as *caractères de
civilité,* he himself called *lettres françaises,* as especially
appropriate to his own country.

Composed by American Book–Stratford Press,
Brattleboro, Vermont

Printed and bound by The Haddon Craftsmen, Inc.,
Scranton, Pennsylvania